CHARLIE MERRICK'S MISFITS

IN FOULS, FRIENDS, & FOOTBALL

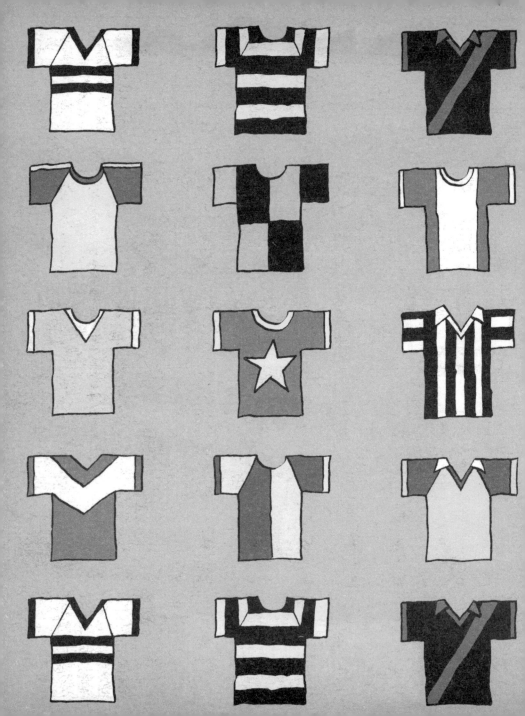

For Mum and Dad.

In memory of
Michael P. Cousins,
who started it all.

OXFORD
UNIVERSITY PRESS

Great Clarendon Street, Oxford, OX2 6DP,
United Kingdom

Oxford University Press is a department of the University of Oxford.
It furthers the University's objective of excellence in research, scholarship,
and education by publishing worldwide. Oxford is a registered trade mark of
Oxford University Press in the UK and in certain other countries

British Library Cataloguing in Publication Data

ISBN: 978-0-19-273659-8

1 3 5 7 9 10 8 6 4 2

Printed and bound by CPI Group (UK) Ltd, Croydon, CR0 4YY

Paper used in the production of this book is a natural,
recyclable product made from wood grown in sustainable forests.
The manufacturing process conforms to the environmental
regulations of the country of origin.

BY DAVE COUSINS

CHARLIE MERRICK'S

MISFITS IN

FOULS, FRIENDS, & FOOTBALL

THIS WAY TO THE ACTION

OXFORD
UNIVERSITY PRESS

WORLD CUP COMPETITION ENTRY FOR:

NORTH ★ GALAXY
UNDER—12s

FOOTBALL—it's all I ever think about. I dream about it when I'm asleep. At school I'm always getting told off for doodling kits and formations. My art teacher says I've got REAL TALENT— I just need to widen my subject matter. So I drew all the away kits to go with the home ones. She wasn't impressed.

WINGER

7

CHARLIE

NAME: CHARLIE MERRICK
SKILLS: Never gives up. Good leader on the pitch. (I'm not being big-headed, that's what our manager, Doug, said!)
NOT SO GOOD AT: Heading; shooting.
★ FACT: Team Captain.

I wish my real talent was football. I can always see the pass or when to make a run into space. The PROBLEM comes when I get the ball. That's when my FEET need to take over. The trouble is, they're NOT QUITE AS GOOD

2

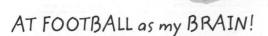

AT FOOTBALL as my BRAIN!

This is my first season as
captain of NORTH STAR GALAXY
UNDER-12s. All our best players left
to join another club, so it's just the subs
and the people nobody else wanted in the team now.
My best mate Sam calls us CHARLIE MERRICK'S
MISFITS—which is about right really!

I'm going to tell you everything that happens—the
TRUTH—however painful that might be. I don't
know how it's going to end. By the time I finish
writing and you finish reading . . . we'll both know!

Charlie Merrick

(team captain)

3

ONE DAY I FOUND THIS.

Edit   View   History   Bookmarks   Windows   Help

Football Factory   X

FAB'S FOO

WHERE FUTURE FOOTBALL STAR

ABOUT • TRAINING ROOM • TACTIC

FAB'S FAB
WORLD CUP
COMPETITION!

IT'S TIME TO
SEIZE
THE
MOMENT

Hi, I'm **FABRICE ROUX**. Playing football was my life, my dream. When injury ended my playing career, I created **FAB'S FOOTBALL FACTORY** to help young players to train better, live a healthy life and enjoy their football.

MY HERO!

BALL FACTORY

Do YOU PLAY youth football?
Would YOUR TEAM like to take part
in a PRE-MATCH TOURNAMENT
at this summer's
WORLD CUP FINALS?
Tell us WHY YOUR TEAM
DESERVES a place at the World Cup.

COMPETITION GUIDELINES:
Are your team record-holding
world-beaters? Or have you battled
against the odds to avoid relegation?
WE WANT YOUR FOOTBALL STORIES.
Send us a video, your club history,
an account of a special game.
Be CREATIVE. Football is about
PASSION, HEART & MAGIC!
Make us LOVE YOUR TEAM
just as much as YOU DO!

PLEASE NOTE: TEAMS MUST
BE BASED IN THE HOST COUNTRY.
CLICK HERE FOR FULL TERMS & CONDITIONS

I READ
THAT . . .

AND
STARTED
THIS.

MATCH REPORT SHEET

NORTH ⭐ GALAXY	V	CEDAR STREET WASPS

FINAL SCORE

0	11

HALF-TIME

0	7

POS	LEAGUE TABLE	PTS
9	LEIGH ROAD COSMOS	3
10	HOLCOMBE WAND	1
11	TORBAY TERRIERS	1
12	NORTH ⭐ GALAXY	0

NORTH ⭐ SQUAD

GK	SAM
D	MOLE
D	MIKO
W	CHARLIE (captain)
DM	DONUT
AM	NATHAN
W	KASH
S	OSCAR
S	LUKAS
SUB	GERBIL

MATCH REPORT

A COMPLETE DISASTER!!!

North Star Galaxy
v
Cedar Street Wasps

There's losing and then there's LOSING! Getting
TROUNCED. BATTERED. HUMILIATED.

Five games. Five defeats. You'd think we'd be used
to it by now . . .

'Eleven—nil!' said Donut. 'ELEVEN!'

'NIL!!' added Gerbil, in case he'd forgotten.

'Remember lads, football's not just about winning,'
said Doug, our manager.

Sam scowled. 'I thought that was the whole point!'

'Well, that's certainly the aim.' Doug scratched
his beard. 'I'd say the POINT is the pure pleasure of
playing the beautiful game!'

If Doug thinks THAT was beautiful, he must have
been watching with his eyes shut.

'How can anyone enjoy losing eleven–nil?' I muttered.

'You want to try being in goal!' said Sam. 'I've never lost count of how many I let in before.'

Jasmine laughed. 'Well, you have only got ten fingers!'

She's allowed to say stuff like that, because every week Jasmine stands on the touchline . . . and watches us lose.

'Right then lads, gather round,' said Doug.

Sam rolled his eyes. 'Here comes the speech.'

No.1 FAN

1

JASMINE

NAME: JASMINE LAWRENCE
SKILLS: Mind Control (Jas can make you do what she wants).
NOT SO GOOD AT: Jas is perfect (see).
★FACT: Me, Sam, & Jas have been friends since Reception, but we're still a bit scared of her!

GOALKEEPER

13

SAM

NAME: SAMSON CHARSLEY (Seriously! His mum's a bit weird.)
SKILLS: Has no fear!
NOT SO GOOD AT: Corners and high shots. Very small for a goalie.
★FACT: Sleeps in his lucky No. 13 shirt the night before every match.

'Hang on, I just need my phone,' I said, digging into my bag.

Doug frowned. 'Do you have to record this, Charlie?'

'It's for the World Cup competition. I need to write down everything that happens. I'll have forgotten what you said by the time I get home!'

9

SUPER SUB

12

GERBIL

NAME: CIARAN MORGAN
SKILLS: Never stops smiling.
NOT SO GOOD AT: Football.
⭐ **FACT:** Gerbil has never scored
a goal, even in training. When he
misses, Gerb shrugs & says 'one
day'. That day is yet to arrive . . .

'You're not still planning to send that in are you?' said Donut. 'We'll never get picked to play at the World Cup if we get thrashed eleven—nil every week!'

'It was only nine last week,' said Gerbil.

Donut snorted.

'Anyway,' I said. 'The history of football is full of teams doing incredible things against the odds, so why not North Star?'

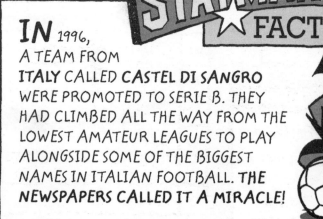

STATMAN ☆ FACT

IN 1996, A TEAM FROM **ITALY** CALLED **CASTEL DI SANGRO** WERE PROMOTED TO SERIE B. THEY HAD CLIMBED ALL THE WAY FROM THE LOWEST AMATEUR LEAGUES TO PLAY ALONGSIDE SOME OF THE BIGGEST NAMES IN ITALIAN FOOTBALL. **THE NEWSPAPERS CALLED IT A MIRACLE!**

MATCH REPORT SHEET

FIVE ACRE V NORTH ⭐ GALAXY

FINAL SCORE

7	2

HALF-TIME

5	0

POS	LEAGUE TABLE	PTS
9	LEIGH ROAD COSMOS	3
10	HOLCOMBE WAND	2
11	TORBAY TERRIERS	2
12	NORTH ⭐ GALAXY	0

NORTH ⭐ SQUAD

GK	SAM		
D	MOLE		
D	MIKO		
W	CHARLIE (captain)		
DM	DONUT		
AM	NATHAN		
W	KASH		
S	OSCAR	⚽⚽	↱
S	LUKAS		
SUB	GERBIL		↱

MATCH REPORT

Another DISASTER! Sam's doing his best, but our DEFENCE has got more holes than a sieve. WE NEED A NEW FORMATION!!!

North Star Galaxy
v
Five Acre

'It's a definite improvement,' said Jasmine, as we walked through the school gates.

'How d'you work that out?' Sam took off his glasses and squinted at Jas.

'Last week you lost eleven—nil, right? Yesterday, it was only seven—two . . . which is half as bad, or twice as good!'

'Seven isn't half of eleven,' said Sam, checking on his fingers.

'No, but Oscar scored two, so you only lost by five—which is actually less than half of eleven.'

'We still lost though,' I said. 'If Doug had listened to my idea for using Donut as a

STRIKER

10

OSCAR

NAME: OSCAR WATTS
SKILLS: Lots! Best player in team.
NOT SO GOOD AT: Not getting fouled—gets injured a lot.
⭐ FACT: Youngest person to win Hardacre Holidaze Holiday Camp 'keepy-uppy' contest, aged 6.

ENEMY No.1

9

TRAVIS

NAME: **TRAVIS JOHNSON**
SKILLS: Boasting. Being an idiot.
NOT SO GOOD AT: Anything else.
⭐ FACT: Ex-North Star Captain.
Moved with his dad (our old
manager) and half the team
to form Goldbridge Colts.

sweeper, we wouldn't have been left wide open at the back again!'

'Sounds painful,' said Jas, laughing.

'It's not funny!'

'So why wouldn't he listen?'

'He said it was too early to start changing things. No need to panic, he said! I'd have thought losing eleven—nil was exactly the time to start panicking!'

We were halfway across the yard when a blonde-haired kid with bushy eyebrows stepped in front of us. 'Well, look who it is! North Star Rejects!' he said, grinning.

'What do you want, Travis?'

'Just wondering how many you lost by yesterday? Thirteen? Twenty?'

'Five, actually,' I said. 'Seven—two, which means we only lost by five!'

13

'Only five! Keep that up and you'll have the whole league quaking in their boots!' He laughed. 'I was just telling Oscar, Colts are top of the league. Six games, six wins. He should come and join us. He's wasted playing with you lot.'

'You keep your hands off Oscar,' said Sam, 'or it'll be you getting wasted!'

Most of the time Sam's really quiet . . . until you get him angry. It's not like he goes green and bursts out of his clothes . . . well, actually, it is a bit like that. Except Sam stays the same size, which is about half as big as anybody he tries to take on.

14

As we dragged Sam away, I couldn't help thinking that eventually Oscar, or someone else, would get fed up of being beaten every week and want to leave. If we lost any more players, North Star would be finished.

And then something happened that changed everything . . .

I was on my way to the canteen at break when Sam appeared, red in the face, and out of breath from running.

'Quick! Got to find him . . . before Travis!'

'Find who?'

'Jack.'

'Who's Jack?'

'New kid,' said Sam, dragging me on to the school field.

I shook myself free. 'Why am I running around the field looking for some kid when I could be inside eating a double-chocolate muffin?'

Sam turned and grabbed my shoulders. 'Before he moved here . . . Jack was at . . . a PREMIERSHIP ACADEMY!'

'What? No way! Did you tell him about North Star?'

Sam slapped his forehead. 'I knew there was something I wanted to talk to him about!' He frowned. 'Of course I did! He was well up for it until Travis barged in and started giving it the North Star Rejects stuff. We've got to find Jack before Travis poaches him for the Golden Turds!'

'Right,' I said, scanning the mass of bodies on the field. 'What's he look like?'

'He's really tall,' said Sam.

I stared at him. 'There are over fifteen hundred kids at this school, and that's the best you can give me?'

Sam shrugged. 'No. REALLY tall!'

In the end, Jack wasn't hard to find. I spotted Travis and his mates circling him like dogs sniffing round a lamp post.

Travis saw us coming. He tried to put an arm round Jack's shoulders, but couldn't reach. It didn't stop the gloating look on his face though—one that told me we were already too late.

'Charlie!' he said. 'Have you met the Colts' new signing?'

'Get lost, Travis!' said Sam. 'I asked him first!'

Travis snorted. 'Wake up, Samson! Why would Jack ever want to play for No Star Tragedy?'

I tried to think of a reason why Jack would be better off playing for a team whose greatest achievement was to lose by only five goals. I could have stood there for the rest of my life ...

WHO'S THAT?

DUNNO, BUT HE'S BEEN THERE SINCE MY GRANDAD WAS AT THIS SCHOOL!

My thoughts were interrupted when someone
tapped me hard on the shoulder. I turned round, and
a girl with long blonde hair thrust a sandwich box
into my stomach.

'You forgot these, brainless,' she snapped. 'I'm
surprised you remember to breathe on your own!'

Everyone turned to watch the girl stalk away, but
it was Jack who spoke.

'Who's that?'

'That sour-faced serpent
of sarcasm,' I sighed, 'is my
sister.'

'Nice,' said Jack.

'You can see where the
quality in your gene pool
went,' said Travis. 'I heard
she's a better footballer
than you, too!'

Now, you're probably
expecting me to engulf
Travis in fiery indignation

SISTER

EMILY

2   N

NAME: EMILY MERRICK
SKILLS: Sarcasm. Being moody.
NOT SO GOOD AT: Minding
her own business.
⭐ FACT: A brilliant footballer.
Captain and leading goalscorer
for Northfield Girls under-14s.

at this latest slur, but I can't. I want this to be a true and accurate record, which means I have to be honest, however painful that might be—and trust me, on the PAIN-O-METER this one is up there with a ball in the family jewels!

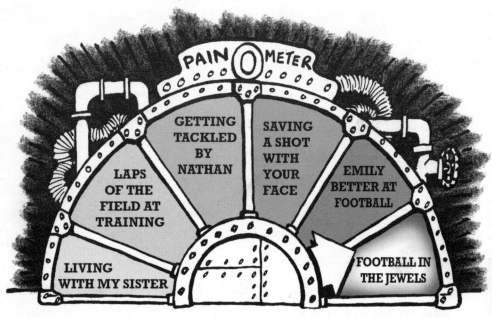

Ok, here goes . . . my sister Emily is a GREAT FOOTBALLER!

There, I've said it. Now, can we PLEASE get back to the action?

'She plays?' said Jack.

I nodded. 'Northfield Girls, under-14s.'

He watched Emily walk across the field, then pulled me to one side. Travis started to follow, but Sam blocked his path.

'Think you could put a word in?' said Jack.

'Eh?'

'With your sister?'

It took me a moment to catch on, because only a lunatic with a death wish would want to go out with my sister!

Jack glanced over his shoulder to where Sam and Travis had started pushing each other. 'Tell you what. You hook me up with your sister, and I'll come and play for North Star.'

It felt like I'd been awarded a penalty in the final minute of a match!

'Deal!' I said, before he changed his mind.

Jack grinned and shook my hand. 'Always choose the team offering the best package,' he said. 'That's what the senior lads at the academy told us!'

Me and Sam couldn't stop grinning . . . and then we told Jasmine.

'You did what?' Jas folded her arms—always a bad sign. 'You can't offer your sister as part of a deal!'

'It was his idea!'

'You didn't have to agree!'

'You don't understand! Jack was at a Premiership academy! This could save North Star!'

'From what?'

'Extinction!'

'And what's going to save you from extinction when Emily finds out?'

Sam laughed. 'You should have seen the look on Travis's face though!'

'I'm more interested in the look on Emily's face, when you tell her,' said Jasmine. 'You don't seriously believe she'll agree to go out with him, do you?'

'She might. If I tell her it's for the good of the team.'

'Trust me,' said Jasmine. 'She won't.'

The smile slipped from Sam's face, the way the ball had escaped his grasp so many times on Sunday. 'But we need him,' he said. 'Charlie will think of something.'

Jasmine snorted. 'Good luck with that one!'

I had a feeling I was going to need a lot more than luck. This was going to take a miracle.

North Star Galaxy
v
Parkview Pirates

Emily was lying on the sofa waiting for the World Cup qualifier between the Republic of Ireland and Germany to start on TV.

'Mum said you scored a great header on Sunday!'

Emily looked up at me. 'What do you want, Charlie?'

'Nothing!' I swallowed. It felt like I was preparing to take a free kick—sizing up the options. I could hear the TV commentators in my head:

Fabrice Roux says that the longer you delay and worry about the kick, the more likely you are to mess it up. The key is to focus on where you want the ball to go, and just hit it. I took a deep breath.

'There's this kid at school. He wants to go out with you.'

There was a moment's silence, then Emily laughed. 'Yeah? Is he hot?'

'Hot?' I hadn't expected that. 'Yeah, of course! Not that I fancy him! I mean, he's a BOY, so why would I? But if I did—fancy boys—which I DON'T, but if I did—I'd probably fancy him.'

Emily sat up. 'I don't suppose you'd say all that again so I can record it on my phone?'

I frowned. 'So . . . what d'you think?'

'I think this is some pathetic attempt at a joke.'

OOH!
THAT'S GONE WAY
OFF TARGET!

'I'm serious!'

'That's even more of a joke,' said Emily. 'Why would I go out with someone who hasn't got the nerve to ask me himself? Seems a bit childish, getting my little brother to do the dirty work.'

'I just said I'd put a word in.'

'You're not doing a very good job, are you?'

I shrugged. 'Um . . . like I said, he's really . . . hot!' I could feel my ears glowing as Emily reached for her mobile. 'He played for one of the Premiership academies before he moved here.'

'Really?' I saw a flicker of interest on Emily's face.

'So, how old is he?'

'Er . . . my year.'

'Your year!' My sister snorted. 'Do you really think I'd go out with someone two years younger than me?'

'He's really tall . . .'

'Forget it, Charlie. If you think he's so hot—you go out with him!' Emily laughed, and turned up the sound on the television.

Thursday Night, Training

'How did you do it?' Sam pulled on his goalkeeping gloves and glanced over to where Jack was talking to Doug.

'I lied. I gave him my mobile number and told him it was Emily's.'

Sam's eyes widened. 'What are you going to do if he calls?'

'Dunno. I'm making this up as I go!' I shrugged. 'As soon as Jack's signed up, I can say Emily changed her mind or something.'

Sam adjusted the Velcro on his gloves and grinned. 'I knew there was a reason Doug made you captain! Come on, last one on the pitch gets MINESWEEPER DUTY!'

Northfield Park is the

only patch of grass for miles around, which means everyone from the houses nearby walks their dogs on our pitch. So, before every game, or training session, we have to minesweep the grass for doggie souvenirs.

At the end of training, Doug let us play a match.

Straight from kick-off, Nathan sped past Kash, then thumped a high pass up to Oscar. As Donut closed in, Oscar slid the ball to Jack. He was unmarked with a clear sight of goal and only Gerbil to beat. He couldn't miss . . .

Two minutes later, Oscar left me for dead and fed Jack another perfect pass. This time, Jack knocked the ball past Gerbil, then ran round to tap it into the empty net. At least that's what he meant to do. Maybe there was a rogue divot in the pitch, or perhaps he got the ball caught up in his feet? Whatever the reason—Jack ended up flat on his back, while the ball dribbled harmlessly into touch.

'It looks like you weren't the only one who was

'lying,' said Sam. 'At least you won't have to worry about Emily now.'

'He sounded so convincing,' I said, 'all that stuff about the academy.'

After ten minutes, Doug blew his whistle and gathered us together.

'Got yourself into some good positions there big man,' he said to Jack. 'On another day you could have had a hat-trick!'

'My mum could have scored a hat-trick tonight,' muttered Nathan.

'Which academy were you at?' said Doug.

'United.'

Doug scratched his chin. 'Striker were you?'

'No, a keeper.'

Which is when everybody stopped and stared at him.

'What did you say?'

Jack dropped his water bottle onto the grass.

'I was youth team goalkeeper.'

'But, you told me you wanted to play up front!'

'I felt like a change.'

Doug frowned. 'Right. Well . . . we normally switch things about a bit in these practice games, so why don't you go in goal for the second half, and Gerbil can have a run-out?'

It didn't take long before Jack was called into action. Nathan barged Miko off the ball and unleashed a rocket towards the top corner of the goal.

For a moment Jack didn't move—then he seemed to unfurl, sprouting extra limbs like an octopus.

One minute the ball was hurtling through the air like a guided missile—the next resting in Jack's hands. He threw it to Kash, who ran round Mole and banged it past Sam while everyone else was still trying to work out what had just happened.

The next time the ball came to me, I deliberately gave it away. I wanted to see if Jack could do it again.

HE DID

AGAIN

AND AGAIN

By the time Doug blew
the final whistle, nobody
had managed to get a single goal past him.

★

I had to run to catch up with Sam.

'That was incredible!' I said.

Sam grunted. 'Did you know he was a keeper?'

'Of course not! He said he wanted to play up front.'

'This is typical,' said Sam. 'I'm back where I started: Sam the Sub!'

'I thought Doug said you could go in defence.'

'I'm a keeper, Charlie! You wouldn't be so pleased if he'd taken your place!'

'It's just for a bit,' I said. 'You'll get to go back in goal.'

'Yeah, right! You said it yourself. Jack's incredible!'

I turned my face away. I felt sorry for Sam, but I couldn't stop grinning at the sensation swelling inside me, like the roar of a crowd as their team sweeps towards the opposition goal. It was a feeling of hope, that maybe, with Jack in the team, North Star had a chance after all.

I need to tell you what happened on the way to the match on Sunday, but my English teacher, Miss O'Malley, says that good writers show you what's happening, rather than just telling you about it. So, that's what I'm going to do. It'll be like you were there, on the other side of the street, listening to every word . . .

OK. I know Miss O'Malley didn't mean we should draw pictures, but it was more fun than writing everything down.

★

When we got to the park, everyone was standing round looking worried.

ARE YOU SURE THEY'RE UNDER-12s?

Parkview is a rough estate on the edge of town. Legend says that if the Pirates don't beat you on the pitch, they beat you up afterwards!

But while everyone else was nervously eyeing the Pirates, I was watching the car park. Jack still hadn't arrived, and kick-off was in less than ten minutes.

Then, just as Sam was about to change into his red goalie's shirt, a sleek black sports car purred into the car park, and Jack climbed out.

Now we'd find out if training had been a fluke, or if Jack really was the miracle North Star needed so desperately.

It took the Pirates exactly twelve seconds to have their first shot. Jack caught it easily, and thumped the ball downfield. It came back moments later with a large pirate attached. I tried, but it was like attempting to tackle a moving train. I picked myself up in time to see the pirate knock the ball past Donut to a kid on the wing. As the return pass looped in towards our area, Sam and the Parkview striker raced to be first to the ball.

The three objects arrived at the same place at exactly the same time. There was a mushy crunch—the sound a chicken might make flying into a brick wall—then the whistle blew, and both teams converged on the wreckage.

SAM

SPLAT!

'That's got to be a card, ref!' said Nathan.

'Fifty-fifty ball,' said the referee, glancing at the black shirts surrounding him.

'You'd better come off so I can check there's nothing broken,' said Doug, crouching over what was left of Sam.

'I'm fine,' said Sam, getting to his feet.

'You sure?'

Sam nodded, and promptly fell down again.

Jack sent the free kick deep into the Pirates' half, but Oscar would have needed a stepladder to beat their centre back to the header. The Parkview number eight collected the ball and thundered towards our goal like a tank. Having seen what had happened to Sam, you couldn't blame Gerbil and Donut for jumping out of the way.

The kid was so sure he'd scored, his arms went up in celebration the moment the ball left his boot . . . but he didn't know about our secret weapon. Jack reached out an arm and plucked the ball from the air as though someone had tossed it gently to him. The Parkview striker stared in amazement.

A minute later it happened again.

And then a third time.

You could almost see the ripple spreading out from Jack's goal, growing stronger with each save. First the Pirates' strikers shaking their heads and shrugging at each other. Slowly it spread doubt through the midfield and into the defence. And, as Parkview began to doubt

42

they were ever going to score, a strange thing happened to the players in blue and yellow: we actually started to believe we might not lose!

With fifteen minutes to go, a long clearance from Jack skimmed off the head of the Parkview centre back, and was intercepted by Oscar. He weaved round one challenge, dodged past another and was about to shoot, when a huge pirate barged him off his feet.

The referee pointed to the penalty spot.

I waited for Oscar to pick up the ball and take the kick. Instead, he turned round and limped towards me.

'That kid gave me a dead leg,' said Oscar. 'You'll have to take it.'

'What?'

Oscar grinned. 'You can do it, Charlie. Win it for us!'

DON'T THINK CHARLIE! PICK YOUR SPOT AND HIT IT! HARD AND LOW.

WIN IT? Moments ago, not losing felt like a victory—winning never crossed my mind. But now we had a chance, and it was all down to ME!

I picked up the ball and wiped it on my shirt.

From this close, the Parkview goalie looked huge and round like an airship. He was jumping about, flapping his arms like he was trying to take off!

I'd never taken a penalty in a real match. What if I blasted it miles over the bar? I could feel panic turning my legs to concrete.

Then, out of nowhere, FABRICE ROUX's voice floated into my head . . .

44

The Pirates barely had time to kick off before the referee blew full time.

'We won!' said Gerbil. 'We actually WON!'

I searched for Sam among the crowd on the touchline.

'He went home,' said Jasmine. 'He wasn't feeling so good.'

'Did he see the goal?'

Jas shook her head.

'What? I can't believe he didn't stay to the end!'

'Maybe he didn't want to listen to everyone going on about how great Jack was,' said Jasmine.

'So what if it was all thanks to Jack? I'd have thought he'd be pleased for the team! That's what's important!'

Jasmine shrugged. 'If you say so.'

For a second I was annoyed with Sam and Jasmine for spoiling the moment, then Gerbil and Oscar jumped on me and started singing one—nil, one—nil, one—nil . . . and I remembered that North Star Galaxy had just recorded their FIRST WIN OF THE SEASON.

FACT

IN 1977-8 BRAZILIAN GOALKEEPER MAZARÓPI SET A WORLD RECORD WHEN HE PLAYED 1,816 MINUTES OF FOOTBALL FOR VASCO DA GAMA WITHOUT CONCEDING A SINGLE GOAL.

OK, I knew Jack had only played one game, but you have to start somewhere!

Weston Road Magpies
v
North Star Galaxy

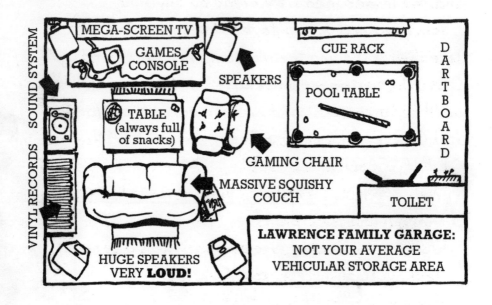

We were sitting in Jasmine's garage waiting for the World Cup qualifier between Jamaica and the USA to start.

'That could be you two soon,' said Jas, as the teams walked out onto the pitch.

'If we do well in the cup we might have a chance.'

Sam looked at me. 'The cup? We win one game and now you're talking about winning the cup!'

'I didn't say WIN IT . . . but why not?' I almost said: With Jack in goal we could do anything.

Sam grunted. 'I'd love to see the look on Travis's face if we did!'

'It's the first round week after next. Do you think you'll be fit by then?'

'How fit do subs need to be?'

'Who says you'll be a sub?'

'Well, after Mr Incredible's performance last week, I'm not going in goal, am I?'

'Doug always makes sure everyone gets a game.'

'Yeah, but not in goal,' said Sam.

There was no answer to that.

'So, Charlie,' said Jasmine, breaking the awkward silence, 'how's your boyfriend?'

'Oh, ha ha!' I frowned. 'I think I might have made Emily sound a bit too keen—Jack won't stop texting.'

'They've got pet names for each other,' said Sam. 'He's JACK RABBIT and Charlie's HONEY BUNNY!'

Jas and Sam started laughing and making gagging noises.

'It's not funny!' I said.

'It won't be when Jack finds out that YOU'RE his little Honey Bunny!' said Jasmine.

'Tell me about it! Emily comes back on Friday!'

'I did warn you,' said Jas. 'You got yourself into this mess. You'll just have to use that genius brain of yours to find a way out.'

On Friday I sent Jack a text explaining that I—Emily—had come down with a bad cold on the trip, and was in bed feeling very unglamorous—which bought me some time. On the way to the match on Sunday, Jack asked how Emily was. I described in horrific detail the snot-monster that had returned from the field trip, hoping it might put him off. Not that it really mattered. I'd already decided that as soon as we got back from the game, Honey Bunny and Jack Rabbit would be history.

MATCH REPORT SHEET

WESTON RD MAGPIES	V	NORTH ⭐ GALAXY

FINAL SCORE

0	0

HALF-TIME

0	0

POS	LEAGUE TABLE	PTS
9	HOLCOMBE WAND	4
10	LEIGH ROAD COSMOS	4
11	TORBAY TERRIERS	4
12	NORTH ⭐ GALAXY	4

NORTH ⭐ SQUAD

GK	JACK
D	MOLE
D	MIKO
W	CHARLIE (captain)
DM	DONUT [1]
AM	NATHAN
W	KASH
S	OSCAR
S	LUKAS [2]
SUBS	SAM [1] & GERBIL [2]

MATCH REPORT

Another CLEAN SHEET
for Jack and another
point for North ⭐.
Still BOTTOM OF THE
LEAGUE though.

'So,' said Jasmine, as we walked into school on Monday. 'Are you single again?'

I nodded. 'I told Jack, I'd—Emily—had met someone new on the field trip.'

'Cruel,' said Sam, laughing. 'Did he cry?'

'No, but he kept asking who it was. Then he . . .'

'What?'

'You don't want to know.'

Jasmine stopped and folded her arms. 'I'm not moving until you tell me.'

I sighed. 'He said . . . he was going to fight for me.'

Sam took his glasses off to wipe the tears from his cheeks.

Jasmine shook her head. 'It's not right playing with people's feelings like that. What are you going to do?'

'I don't know.'

'You might want to think of something,' said Sam, 'because he's coming over now.'

Jack said he wanted a private word, then started interrogating me about Emily's new boyfriend.

'You need to find out who it is,' he said, leaning over me. 'Nobody steals my woman and gets away with it!'

Did he have to be so dramatic? Couldn't he just lock himself in his bedroom and listen to miserable music for a few days, like everyone else who got dumped?

'Or maybe I'll ask her myself!' said Jack.

I looked up and saw Emily crossing the yard.

'NO!' I stepped in front of him. 'Not a good idea! Let me talk to her! If you get on the wrong side of her now, you'll have no chance. Trust me—I'll sort it.'

Jack grunted. 'You'd better, or the deal's off.'

'What? It's not my fault she found someone else.'

'Just sort it!' said Jack.

Before I could say anything else, Travis slithered up to us. 'Still doing charity work then, I see,' he said, clapping Jack on the back. 'No Star haven't lost since you joined.'

I glared at him. 'Did you want something, Travis?'

'Just to remind Jack that when he's ready to play for a proper team, there's a place for him with Colts.'

'I'm giving North Star a chance,' said Jack, giving me a meaningful look. 'Right, Charlie?'

I nodded. 'Right.'

They do say that true love never dies . . .

DISTRICT CUP ROUND ONE:

Witchmore Junction B
v
North Star Galaxy

STATMAN FACT

DENMARK DIDN'T QUALIFY FOR THE **1992 EUROPEAN CHAMPIONSHIPS,** BUT GOT A PLACE WHEN YUGOSLAVIA COULDN'T TAKE PART. THEY WENT ON TO WIN—BEATING GERMANY IN THE FINAL! PROVING THAT **SOMETIMES THE TEAM NOBODY EXPECTS COMES OUT ON TOP!**

North Star were still bottom of the league, but the cup gave us a chance to prove we weren't just a team of rejects and no-hopers.

Witchmore Junction were in Division One, and had entered two teams for the cup. We'd been drawn against their B-team—which meant, like us, they had a point to prove. For the first twenty minutes the ball barely left our half. Luckily, Jack was on top form—happy now that he and Honey Bunny were back together, and had a date fixed for that very evening. Unfortunately, that fact was having the opposite effect on my performance. I was up against the Witchmore number three: a skinny, dark-haired kid, who managed to find a new way to make me look stupid every time he got the ball.

But, on the rare occasions we managed to cross the halfway line, things started to look more hopeful. The Witchmore defence was worse than ours—all of them had a tendency to run towards the player with the ball, leaving everyone else unmarked. I pointed this out to Oscar, and five minutes later he lured all three defenders out wide, then chipped the ball to Nathan. He couldn't miss.

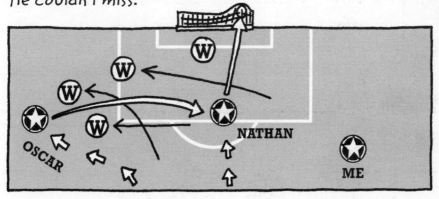

The Witchmore coach was furious. His team responded with wave after wave of attacks, but they couldn't get past Jack.

With ten minutes to go, Witchmore got a corner. Having seen their last two plucked from the air by our octopus goalkeeper, they played it short, then whacked a cross into the crowded penalty area. Donut yelped as the ball smacked against his thigh and rolled towards ME and the NUMBER THREE.

'Unlucky, Charlie!' Donut helped me up. 'They were bound to score eventually.'

'Yeah, but THEY didn't. I DID!'

'Could have happened to anyone,' said Jack. 'Don't worry about it.'

But I couldn't stop worrying. We'd been so close, and I'd blown it.

Five minutes later Doug brought Gerbil on in my place.

'Not your fault, mate. Just not going well for you today!' He patted me on the back.

I nodded, and sat down behind the touchline, praying we would hold on. If the scores were level at the end of a cup game, the tie would be settled by a penalty shoot-out. With Jack in goal, we had a real chance.

Doug had waved everyone back to defend, and when the ball fell to Oscar on the edge of our penalty box I expected him to hoof it away. Instead, he started running. I think the Witchmore players were as surprised as me, because Oscar had reached the halfway line before any of them decided to follow him . . . by which time it was too late.

As Oscar reached the edge of the penalty box, the goalkeeper darted forward and made a desperate dive for the ball . . . but it was already in the air, curling over his head into the net.

Witchmore had just enough time to kick off and send a hopeful punt towards our goal, before the final whistle sounded. We'd won. North Star were in the next round of the cup!

'What's up with you today?' said Sam, as we got changed. 'Worried about your big date tonight?'

'Keep your voice down!' I looked over to where Jack was pulling his tracksuit on.

'So, what you going to do? Dress up in your sister's clothes and a wig?' He laughed.

'I don't need to dress up. Emily's going to be there.'

'What? She agreed to go out with Jack?'

'Not exactly. I told Emily I'd pay for us to go and see the new Todd Tempest film. Then I sent a text to Jack—as Emily—arranging to meet him there too.'

Sam frowned. 'So Emily thinks she's going to the film with you—and Jack thinks he's going with Emily—which is also you!' His eyes widened. 'That means Jack and Emily are going to actually meet!'

'That's kind of how a date works.'

'Yeah, but what happens when Jack walks up to Emily and says:

HONEY BUNNY! GIVE US A KISS!

GRRRRR

That same nightmare scenario had occurred to me, but I was doing my best to ignore it.

'I'll make sure we get there late, so there's no time for chat.'

Sam shook his head. 'It won't work. You've been lucky so far, but even you won't pull this one off.'

I shrugged. 'It's worth a try. Like Fabrice Roux says: if you don't shoot, you'll never score!'

'I know you're up to something,' said Emily. 'But I'm not turning down a free trip to the cinema.' She pointed a finger at me. 'Remember—large popcorn and ice cream—that was the deal!'

I spotted Jack the moment we walked through the doors.

'Hey, look, there's Jack!' I said, thrusting a twenty-pound note into my sister's hand. 'You get the snacks.'

Emily looked like she was about to protest, then saw how much money I'd given her. 'Don't expect any change,' she said, and walked away.

'What you doing here?' said Jack, glancing towards Emily.

'Mum and Dad wouldn't let her come on her own,' I said. 'I'm here to make sure you don't get up to anything . . . you know . . . funny.'

'Funny?' Jack frowned.

'Don't worry. You won't even know I'm here.'

Jack didn't look convinced, but then his skills lay between the posts of a football goal—off the field, he wasn't the brightest kid I'd ever met.

I pulled another note from my pocket and handed it to Jack. 'Why don't you go and get the tickets while I give Emily a hand with the snacks. My treat!'

Jasmine had said I would have to pay for my deception—she wasn't wrong. I'd been saving for weeks to get the new edition of Pro Soccer on the PlayStation, but this was more important.

'Guess what?' I said, joining Emily in the queue for popcorn. 'Jack Rabbit's here to see the same film. I said he could sit with us.'

'Jack Rabbit?'

'It's what we call him.'

'Sad!' Emily shook her head. 'Just make sure you don't talk all the way through.'

'You can sit in the middle, then we won't be able to,' I said. 'Oh, by the way, if Jack calls you HONEY BUNNY—it's just a northern thing—he does it to everyone.'

Emily looked at me. 'If anyone calls ME Honey Bunny, they'll be eating hospital food for a week.'

Jack was waiting by the barrier.

'Hello, Jack Rabbit,' said Emily, her voice dripping with sarcasm.

But Jack didn't seem to notice. He stared at her, pale-faced and silent—like a startled rabbit! Then I realized what was wrong: for all his talk and swagger, when faced with a real live girl, the mighty Jack Rabbit was struck dumb with fear!

'Right,' I said. 'Shall we go in?'

Moments after we sat down, the lights dimmed and the trailers flickered onto the screen. I glanced to my left, past Emily, to where Jack was sitting bolt upright, clutching the arms of his seat like he was on a roller-coaster. I wondered if this was the first time he'd ever been out with a girl, let alone someone two years older than him.

An advert for the World Cup came on: stirring music over slow-motion images of spectacular goals and crunching tackles. Each thump of boot against ball echoed in my chest as crowd noise swirled around the cinema, and the slogan SEIZE THE MOMENT! flashed on screen. I was so engrossed, I forgot about the potential own-goal waiting in the seats to my left.

It happened twenty minutes into the film. Emily swore, then jumped up like she'd been electrocuted.

'What's going on?' I said, as people around us started complaining.

'He tried to grope me!' hissed Emily, demanding we swap places.

I shuffled into the seat next to Jack. 'What did you do?'

He didn't answer—just bolted for the exit.

I caught up with him outside. 'Jack! What happened?'

His face was bright red. He looked at the ground and shrugged. 'I just put my arm round her and she completely freaked out!'

'Ah . . . that's my sister for you! One minute, nice as anything—the next, ripping your throat out for no reason at all!' I laughed.

'She was so different on text,' said Jack. 'It's like she doesn't know me!' He frowned. 'You won't tell anyone about this, will you?'

'Course not!' He looked so miserable, I actually

started to feel a bit guilty. 'Your secret's safe with me! See you at training, yeah?'

Jack nodded, then turned and headed home.

BRIAN STATLER AT HARDACRE CINEMA

WHAT A RESULT!
THE BIG LAD HANDED
THAT TO OUR BOY
ON A PLATE.
TALK ABOUT LUCKY!

Shutt Lane Monarchs
v
North Star Galaxy

I was worried that the end of the doomed love affair between Jack Rabbit and Honey Bunny might damage Jack's ability in goal. If anything, it had the opposite effect. The following Sunday he inspired the team to a three—one victory, and North Star moved off the bottom of the league for the first time!

The next game was against Shutt Lane Monarchs, who were two places above us in the table. If we beat them, we could go as high as seventh!

The players gathered in the car park for the trip to Shutt Lane were almost unrecognizable as the team who had lost eleven—nil just a few weeks earlier.

'When's the Goldbridge game again?' said Oscar.

'Next month,' I told him.

'I can't wait to stick one on them,' said Nathan.

Gerbil grinned. 'Hey! Reckon we'll be top of the league by Christmas!'

'Let's not get carried away,' said Doug, handing out directions to the Monarchs' ground. 'How about we concentrate on winning this game, before you start clearing space for the championship trophy.'

Jack's dad looked at the sheet he'd been given.

'Er, Doug, what's the postcode, mate? I'll put it in my sat nav.'

'You won't need that,' said Doug. 'Just follow us. These are in case we get separated. Right, who's with me?'

Which was the signal for CAR ROULETTE to begin. You see, travel to away games depended on whose parents were available with transport. It usually came down to the same four options— some good—some not so good . . .

Transportation options for away games:

The BEAST

Rating: ★★☆☆☆

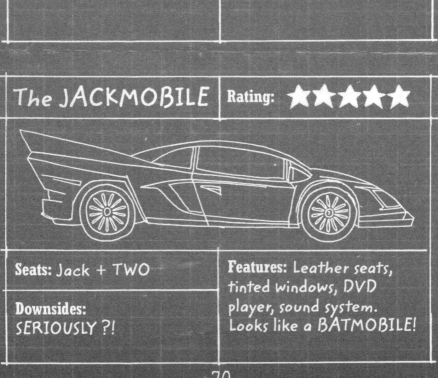

Features:
You get to wear a crash helmet and leather jacket.

Downsides:
Only Nathan is allowed to travel on his dad's bike.

Seats available:
ONE (for Nathan)

The JACKMOBILE

Rating: ★★★★★

Seats: Jack + TWO

Downsides:
SERIOUSLY ?!

Features: Leather seats, tinted windows, DVD player, sound system.
Looks like a BATMOBILE!

The BARBIE CAR

Rating: ★★★☆☆

Features:
If you can't get a seat in the JACKMOBILE, this is the next best option.

Seats available:
Gerbil + TWO

Downsides:
Having to sit next to Gerbil's little sister, Sian, and play Barbie.

The HEARSE

Rating: ★☆☆☆☆

Downsides:
We call it the HEARSE because: a) it smells like something died in there; b) Doug plays music by old bands who are all dead; c) Doug's mind wanders while he's driving, so you're risking your life every journey.

Seats: Donut + THREE

Features:
Better than walking!

When the convoy finally rolled out of the car park it was Kash and Oscar who had won the right to travel in style. Sam and I had bagged the Barbie seats, while this week's losers—Lukas, Miko, and Mole— joined Donut in the Hearse.

We stopped at the junction by the cinema where Jack Rabbit and Honey Bunny's infamous date had taken place, but the moment the lights changed, the Jackmobile slipped past like a shadow, and vanished into the distance.

'Doug won't like that,' said Gerbil's mum, Molly.

'He's got sat nav,' said Gerbil. 'In fact, that thing's probably got an autopilot!'

The moment we arrived at Shutt Lane Sports Club I knew something was wrong. Doug sprang out of the Hearse and dived into the boot, while Donut and the others stood round looking worried.

'What's up?'

'Um,' said Donut. 'We can't find the kit.'
'We can't find the kit, because SOMEBODY didn't put it in the car!' Doug emerged clutching a black bin-liner. 'You'll have to wear these.'

'I'm sorry,' said Doug, 'but it's all we've got. At least they've got numbers on the back.'
'What's a HEN PASTY?' said Sam.

'It should say PARTY. Nobody noticed until we printed them. That's why they were in the back of the car.'

'NO WAY am I wearing THAT!' said Nathan.

'Um . . . I think we might have a bigger problem,' I said. 'Has anyone seen the Jackmobile?'

The referee came over and pointed to his watch. 'We can't wait much longer—there's another game on this pitch at twelve.'

Doug nodded and scanned the car park for the hundredth time, but there was still no sign of the Jackmobile.

'Right lads,' he said. 'Monarchs have agreed to play eight v eight. Gerbil, you're our lone striker, so I want Charlie, Nathan and Lukas to push up when we've got the ball. Sam, you're in goal.'

Sam looked happier than I'd seen him in weeks.

Doug clapped his hands. 'Three wins. Unbeaten in four. Just go out there and do what you've been doing.'

Nobody said it, but we were all thinking the same thing. So was Doug, you could tell by the way he kept glancing hopefully towards the car park. Those results had all come with Jack in goal. What were we going to be like without him?

We almost scored straight from kick-off. Shutt Lane Monarchs were laughing so hard at our shirts they could barely stand, let alone play football.

Unfortunately the chance fell to Gerbil, whose shot was so high the ball sailed out of the ground and a new one had to be fetched. The brief interruption in play was our best moment of the half.

The entire team had gone back to playing like we did before Jack joined, and couldn't string two passes together. The fact we were only three down at half-time was thanks to some great goalkeeping by Sam.

And there was still no sign of the others.

They finally arrived five minutes into the second half, with Jack's dad muttering about SAT NAV and the WRONG Shutt Lane. Doug made three immediate substitutions: Oscar for Gerbil; Kash for Nathan; and Jack for Sam, who tore off his gloves and threw them over the touchline.

Commentators talk about a game of two halves; this was a game of TWO TEAMS! Shutt Lane didn't know what had hit them. With Jack back in goal, everyone started to play better. Miko actually made a tackle, then found Oscar with a long-range pass. Our star striker danced through the Monarchs' defence and slammed the ball into the net.

ONE—THREE.

They were still reeling when Donut headed the second. One more, and we'd be level.

But it wouldn't come. Kash dribbled through a crowd of players only to find the goalkeeper blocking his path; Oscar had one cleared off the line; even I managed to hit the post! We just couldn't SCORE!

The referee had already checked his watch when we won a corner.

I ran over to take it. We had minutes, maybe seconds to go. This was our last chance.

I looked for a target among the players crowding the goal, but with Nathan off the pitch, we were dwarfed by the Shutt Lane defenders. Then I had a genius idea.

'Jack!' I signalled to the lone figure in our goal.

'Come on, lad!' The referee pointed to his wrist.

I waved again. Finally Jack understood and started running. Jack, who was head and shoulders above everyone else on the pitch. Now ALL I had to do was get the corner on target. My last attempt hadn't even beaten the first defender.

> YOU CAN DO IT, CHARLIE. REMEMBER TO LEAN BACK AS YOU HIT IT!

Somehow—maybe luck, or the divine intervention of Fabrice Roux— I got it right. All Jack had to do was nod the ball into the net, and we were level—THREE-ALL.

'Not only is he keeping them out at one end, he's scoring at the other!' said Nathan's dad, as we came off the pitch.

'Great comeback lads!' said Doug. 'Thank God you made it in time!'

Sam was sitting on his own, tearing chunks of grass from between his feet. I walked over and sat down next to him.

'Talk about last minute, eh?'

Sam snorted.

'You were brilliant in the first half,' I said. 'We'd never have got back more than three.'

'Don't bother,' said Sam.

'What?'

'You're just trying to make me feel better.'

'I'm not. You were great!'

Sam looked at me, and I could see tears in his eyes. 'But I'm not as good as him, am I? I'll always be a sub while he's here.' He stood up. 'I've had enough. I'm leaving.'

'What?'

'North Star don't need me. So what's the point?'

I watched Sam stomp towards the car park and suddenly felt angry. Why did he have to spoil everything? I understood why he felt bad, but he was just thinking about himself—not the team. Since Jack joined, we hadn't lost a match. We were ninth in the league! If this carried on, who knew what we might achieve . . .

HAVE YOU TALKED TO HIM YET?

I TALK TO SAM ALL THE TIME.

YOU NEED TO TALK TO HIM ABOUT NORTH STAR.

I TRIED.

HE WON'T CHANGE HIS MIND.

HEY, THIS IS GONNA BE ONE FAT SNOWMAN!

CHARLIE!

YOU MANAGED TO TRICK JACK INTO PLAYING.

BUT YOU'RE TELLING ME YOU CAN'T PERSUADE YOUR BEST FRIEND TO COME BACK?

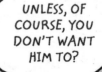

UNLESS, OF COURSE, YOU DON'T WANT HIM TO?

DISTRICT CUP ROUND TWO:

North Star Galaxy
v
Harperstown Albion

Thursday Night, Training

The wind whipped across the park, slapping any exposed patch of skin into a burning numbness as we gathered round Doug in the goalmouth.

'I can't feel my toes,' said Gerbil. 'What if they've fallen off? What if, when I take my boots off, there's just a stump and five toes in the bottom of my sock? I might never play again.'

'What a loss to football that would be,' said Nathan.

'Right!' said Doug, clapping his hands. 'It's the CUP on Sunday, so we're going to do some shooting practice. Who wants to go in goal?'

Doug wasn't exactly knocked over by a rush of people volunteering to throw themselves around on the frozen ground while the rest of the team fired footballs at them—so, as usual, he picked Donut.

'Why isn't Jack here?' said Donut, pulling on the spare goalkeeping gloves.

'He's not as stupid as us,' said Oscar.

'He's so good he doesn't need to train,' said Gerbil.

'Nobody's too good for training,' Doug said. 'If Jack wants to be part of this team, he should be here. The rest of you made the effort.'

'Some of us need all the practice we can get,' said Nathan, giving Gerbil a nudge.

'I'm getting better!' said Gerbil. 'Anyway, I've got a good feeling about the cup match. I reckon it could be my day. If I've got any toes left by then!'

Harperstown Albion were third in Division One. As we were still in the bottom half of Division Two, their manager had obviously decided they could afford to rest their first team and let some of the fringe players have a go. He clearly hadn't heard about Jack, or Oscar. By the time he realized his mistake, we were two—nil up.

Albion made six substitutions and pulled a goal back almost immediately. For the next half an hour we defended, employing a tactic known as PARKING THE BUS!

The Harperstown manager was going crazy, complaining to the referee that we weren't even trying, but there's nothing in the rules

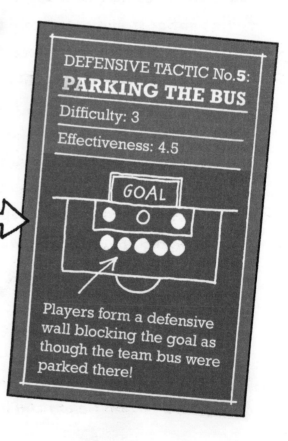

DEFENSIVE TACTIC No.5:
PARKING THE BUS
Difficulty: 3
Effectiveness: 4.5

GOAL

Players form a defensive wall blocking the goal as though the team bus were parked there!

to say you can't form a human shield around your goal. The Albion players took it in turns trying to hammer the ball over, around, or simply through, the barrier of blue and yellow.

With ten minutes to go, the Harperstown goalkeeper decided he was getting lonely and came up to join the shooting practice. His first attempt thumped into Donut's stomach and bounced in front of Gerbil, who gave it an almighty hoof downfield. Except now, there wasn't anybody in the Albion half to kick it back. For the first time in his life, Gerbil's ability to kick a football into orbit actually worked in his favour. Three of the Albion players raced after it, including a very red-faced goalkeeper, but they didn't stand a chance. The ball bounced twice

.. . bobbled

.. . rolled

.. . and finally trickled over the line into the empty goal. The Albion manager buried his head in his hands. Three-one.

In the last minute Harperstown made it three—two and for a moment I thought they were going to equalise, but the BUS and Jack stood firm.

When the whistle finally blew, Gerbil sank to the ground and lay back with his arms outstretched. 'Charlie!' he said, eyes wide in disbelief. 'We're through to the quarter-final! And I scored the winner!'

'Total fluke!' said Nathan, dragging Gerbil to his feet. 'Could have gone anywhere!'

'No way! I told you I'd score!'

'Yeah! Guess you did.' Nathan grinned and hoisted Gerbil onto his shoulders, then ran round the pitch while Gerbil shrieked that he was scared of heights and begged to be put down.

Thursday Night, Training

I was worried. Ever since the trip to the cinema, Jack had been avoiding me. He'd also started sitting with the Colts in the canteen at school. Now he'd missed training for the second week running. Doug wasn't happy. With no Jack or Sam, Donut and Gerbil went in goal for the practice game. They were hopeless. If we had to use either of them for a real match, we were doomed.

FACT

NOT ALL OUTFIELD PLAYERS ARE RUBBISH IN GOAL! IN THE FINAL MINUTES OF A **UEFA CUP** MATCH AGAINST **AS NANCY** IN 2006, **FC BASEL GOALKEEPER FRANCO COSTANZO** GAVE AWAY A PENALTY AND WAS SENT OFF. THE TEAM HAD ALREADY USED THEIR THREE SUBS, SO **STRIKER MLADEN PETRIĆ WENT IN GOAL AND SAVED THE PENALTY!**

North Star Galaxy
v
Dirkhill Dynamos

When I arrived at the park on Sunday morning, Jack and Sam were both there.

'What's going on?'

'Doug's dropped Jack and put Sam in goal!' Oscar shook his head.

'You all know the rule,' said Doug. 'If you don't train, you don't play.'

'I thought Sam left?' I looked over to where Sam was warming up.

'He did,' said Doug. 'But I asked him to give us another chance. Sam lost his place when Jack arrived, but he still came to training—and played in defence when I asked him to.'

'Yeah, but we need Jack! Without...'

Doug cut me off. 'I've made my decision, Charlie. If Jack wants his place back, he'll have to earn it.'

We were a goal down in less than a minute.

It wasn't Sam's fault the Dynamos' striker was allowed to stroll unchallenged through our defence and pick his spot.

We were all over the place—sliced passes, mistimed tackles—all Dirkhill had to do was wait for us to give the ball away.

I was standing near the touchline when

Miko air-kicked a clearance, allowing the Dynamos' striker to blast the ball past Sam for the second goal.

Doug threw up his hands in despair. 'What's wrong with them?'

'It's Jack,' I said.

'But Jack's not even on the pitch!'

'He's good luck!' said Gerbil. 'When Jack's in goal, we just feel more confident.'

Doug ran a hand through his non-existent hair. 'But he never comes to training. It doesn't seem fair.'

'I don't think anyone minds if we keep winning,' I said.

There was a cheer from the opposite touchline, and I looked up in time to see Sam picking the ball out of the net for the third time.

Doug sighed and shook his head. 'OK, I'll put Jack on at half-time.'

'Um, Doug,' said Gerbil.

'Yes, I'll put you on too, Gerbil.'

'I didn't mean that,' said Gerbil. 'I was going to tell you that Jack's already gone home.'

The less said about the rest of the game, the better. The report sheet tells you all you need to know.

MATCH REPORT SHEET

NORTH  GALAXY	V	DIRKHILL DYNAMOS

FINAL SCORE

1	6

HALF-TIME

0	4

POS	LEAGUE TABLE	PTS
9	NORTH ☆ GALAXY	8
10	TORBAY TERRIERS	5
11	LEIGH ROAD COSMOS	5
12	HOLCOMBE WAND	4

NORTH ☆ SQUAD

GK	SAM
D	MOLE
D	MIKO
W	CHARLIE (captain)
DM	DONUT [1]
AM	NATHAN
W	KASH
S	OSCAR
S	LUKAS
SUBS	GERBIL [1] & JACK*

*(until he went home!)

MATCH REPORT

At least the teams below us lost too—so we're still 9th in the league. But if it carries on like THIS, we

We all assumed that Doug would put Jack back in
goal for the next match.

WRONG!

He was so angry that Jack had gone home early,
Sam kept his place for the disastrous trip to Mayfield
Borough. If you want the gory details, here's
the match report:

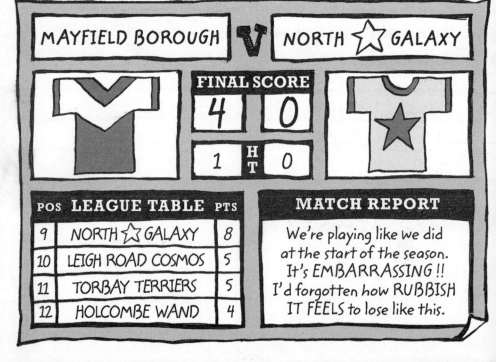

| MAYFIELD BOROUGH | V | NORTH ☆ GALAXY |

FINAL SCORE

4 — 0

1 — HT — 0

POS	LEAGUE TABLE	PTS
9	NORTH ☆ GALAXY	8
10	LEIGH ROAD COSMOS	5
11	TORBAY TERRIERS	5
12	HOLCOMBE WAND	4

MATCH REPORT

We're playing like we did
at the start of the season.
It's EMBARRASSING!!
I'd forgotten how RUBBISH
IT FEELS to lose like this.

With the Colts match coming up, Travis wouldn't leave me alone.

'So, this must be the losers' table,' he said, pausing on his way across the canteen. 'I'm thinking twenty.'

'What are you on about?'

'Colts put ten past Torbay Terriers last week, but I'm thinking twenty against you lot.'

I shrugged.

'I can't believe that idiot manager of yours dropped Jack. Hilarious!' Travis laughed. 'Oh, by the way, did I mention Colts are playing at the World Cup?'

'What?'

He grinned. 'Nothing definite yet, but I'd say with our one hundred per cent record, it's in the bag. Ciao!'

I pushed away the remains of my lunch.

Suddenly, I wasn't hungry.

Goldbridge Colts
v
North Star Galaxy

They were laughing as we climbed out of the Hearse.

'Hey, look, it's the rejects!'

'I thought they'd been thrown out of the league for being rubbish.'

'After today, they'll be begging to get chucked out!'

'I remember when North Star Galaxy were good. Oh, yeah, that was when we played for them!'

Doug kept a firm grip on Sam and herded us into the changing room before a fight broke out. Notice I said CHANGING ROOM! No getting ready at the side of the pitch, or in the car park, for the Colts. They had a shiny new clubhouse. It was a bit different from our hut.

SPOT THE DIFFERENCE: See how many differences you can find!

'We're doomed,' said Donut, pointing to a sheet of paper stuck to the changing-room wall.

GOLDBRIDGE COLTS
PLAYED 12
WON 12
TODAY No.13
UNLUCKY FOR SOMEONE!

Doug ripped it down. 'This,' he said, 'and that nonsense outside. You can use it! Who do they think they are, laughing at us? I say, we go out there and wipe the smiles off their smug faces!'

I'd never seen Doug so angry and fired up.

'Um ...' Gerbil raised a shaking hand. 'How are we supposed to do that, exactly?'

But before Doug could answer, a noise rumbled

through the wall from the Colts' dressing room—
the word COLTS being chanted over and over,
accompanied by stamping feet and fists pounding
on wooden benches.

'What are they doing in there?' said Donut, his
eyes widening in horror.

'Winding you up,' said Doug. He had to shout to
be heard over the racket. 'Listen! I want you to go
out there and get in their faces right from the start.
Stay tight. Don't give them space to play. They're
expecting us to just roll over and die. I say we give
them a surprise!'

'Yeah!' growled Nathan, grinning in a way that
made me glad he was on my side.

'Let's give these idiots a game to remember,' said
Oscar.

After that, we couldn't wait to get started. As we
ran out onto the pitch, I actually thought we might
have a chance.

The moment Colts kicked off, Nathan pounced and powered into their half before they realized what was happening. As the first tackle came in, he switched the ball wide to me. I took two strides, then thumped it to Oscar, who turned and shot so quickly the goalkeeper didn't even move. The ball flew past him, pinged against the post and rebounded into play.

There was no time to think about how close we had come to taking the lead. A sea of white shirts flooded towards us, and thirty seconds after Oscar had hit the woodwork at one end, Travis slammed the ball against Sam's post. Except this time, it didn't come out again.

'No way!' Donut flung his arms to the sky.

'Luck!' I said. 'We almost scored, we can do it again.'

But this time the Colts were ready, and got the ball before we were anywhere near their goal. We did what Doug had told us, closing them down, frustrating them with sheer numbers of blue and yellow shirts. Each time they did break through, Sam managed to get a part of his body in the way and keep the ball out. Incredibly, at half-time the score was still only one—nil.

'Just keep doing what you're doing,' said Doug. 'You'll get another chance.'

Early in the second half, the Colts got a corner. As the ball came over, Nathan jumped to head it away, and the Colts' number seven tumbled to the ground.

'I never touched him!' said Nathan, when the referee pointed to the penalty spot.

The number seven got to his feet, and winked at Travis.

So that was how they were going to play it!

From that moment on, every time a blue shirt got too close, or—horror of horrors, dared to make a tackle—the player in white would fling himself to the ground and roll round in agony.

Before long, half our team had been booked, and we had no choice but to back off. The injustice of it all undid us, and five minutes later the Colts were three-up. Then Travis put the ball through Mole's legs and blasted a fourth past Sam. By full time they'd scored nine—not even halfway to Travis's promised twenty, but it was no consolation.

I got changed quickly, and found Doug wrestling a bag of footballs into the back of the Hearse.

'You've got to put Jack in goal for the cup,' I said.

Doug closed the boot. 'It's not Sam's fault we lost today!'

'I know, Sam was brilliant, but it's like Gerbil said, the rest of us play better when Jack's there.'

'He's not a lucky charm, Charlie!'

'Yeah, but we've never lost with him in the team.'

'So you want me to drop Sam—your best mate—and put Jack in goal for the quarter-final?' Doug looked at me.

'I'm just thinking what's best for the team.'

He sighed. 'Why don't you let me worry about what's best for the team?'

And there was the problem. Don't get me wrong—Doug's great, but he just doesn't get it. Nobody cared if Jack came to training. We just wanted him in goal. We'd had a taste of not getting beaten every week, and we liked it. We'd actually started to believe in ourselves, and it had all been thanks to Jack.

If Doug wasn't going to listen to reason, I'd have to think of something else.

It took less
than a minute
to bike up to
Sam's house,
but that was
long enough
for the idea
to materialize
in my head, like a
wisp of black smoke
with horns and a
forked tail.

I shook it away. I couldn't do that!

As I sat on my bike, staring across the street at my best friend's house, a bus grumbled along the road throwing squares of light across the pavement. There was an advert plastered across the back.

WORLD CUP TICKETS ON SALE NOW.

IT'S TIME TO SEIZE THE MOMENT

I watched the bus turn onto the main
road, then looked back at the house. The
light in Sam's bedroom glowed behind the
curtains, but the idea had taken shape again,
growing more solid until
I couldn't see past it.

I turned my bike around and pedalled away.

DISTRICT CUP QUARTER FINAL:

Cedar Street Wasps
v
North Star Galaxy

Doug counted the players packed into the minibus and frowned. 'You definitely told Sam nine o'clock?'

'Well, nobody answered when I knocked, so I put a note through the door.'

'You did what?'

'I didn't know what else to do!'

Doug looked at his watch and swore under his breath. 'We can't wait any longer. Looks like you're in goal today, Donut.'

There was a collective groan from the rest of the team, then Oscar pointed through the back window. 'Hang on, someone's coming.'

'You're cutting it fine, Sam ...' said Doug, as the rear door opened.

But it was Jack who climbed into the bus.

'I thought you might need a sub,' he said, sliding into the empty seat next to me.

'We do, as it happens,' said Doug, giving me a suspicious glance.

I looked away. If Doug had listened to me in the first place, I wouldn't have had to take such drastic measures.

The moment Jack arrived, the mood inside the bus changed from despair to elation. Oscar and Gerbil started making bets on how many goals we would win by, and who we'd get in the semi-final. But knowing I was right didn't shift the guilt sitting in my stomach like undigested breakfast.

As the bus pulled out on to the main road, Jack nudged me. 'Let's have it then?'

I checked nobody was watching, then handed him a blue and yellow sock.

'Inside,' I whispered. 'I thought a brown envelope was a bit obvious.'

Jack grunted and shoved the sock into his bag.

'Fifty?'

I nodded. Fifty quid. All my Christmas money, but it was worth it.

The Cedar Street pitch was at the bottom of a steep hill. The ground sloped so dramatically that if Oscar stood on one wing, he was taller than Nathan on the other.

SO THAT'S WHAT THE TOP OF NATHAN'S HEAD LOOKS LIKE.

'Keep it simple until you get a feel for the slope,' said Doug. 'Wasps will be used to it, so they're going to have an advantage.'

'No wonder they're second in the league,' said Kash.

'Yeah, but we've got Jack!' Gerbil grinned.

Which was the cue for Doug to give me another dirty look. For a moment I thought he might insist on the no-train, no-play rule, but he probably realized there would be a riot if he left Jack out again.

We started with the slope on our right, which meant I was halfway up the hill. Most of the passes aimed for me never made it up the incline, while all my crosses sailed miles too high. Meanwhile, the Wasps swarmed round us with ease.

But they couldn't beat Jack.

Slowly, as the Wasps became more frustrated, we got used to the pitch. Oscar hit the post, and Kash brought a great save from their keeper, but at half-time it was still nil—nil.

Ten minutes into the second half we got a corner.
It was uphill. I'd need to give this a good whack. But
as my foot connected, I leaned back and, straight
away, knew I'd overdone it. The ball flew miles over
the crowd of waiting players.

And then I saw Oscar—
High up on the opposite touchline—
The smallest player on the pitch.

He ran . . .

jumped . . .

And headed the ball into the net!

For the rest of the game, the Wasps didn't leave
our half, but they still couldn't beat Jack.

All round me
the team were hugging.
We'd done it! North Star were through
to the SEMI-FINAL. I should have felt amazing,
so why did I feel so bad?

'Sam called me from a phone box just after
kick-off,' said Doug, taking me to one side.
'Reckoned he didn't know the time had changed.'

'Maybe he didn't see the note.'

'No, he didn't. In fact, Sam couldn't find it
anywhere.'

I shrugged. 'It must have gone under a table or something.'

'Gone under a table?' Doug exhaled slowly. 'So, Sam missing the bus and then Jack just happening to turn up, was all a coincidence?'

'Yeah.'

Doug held my gaze for so long my eyes began to water. 'I hope for your sake it was, Charlie . . . because if I'd engineered something like that, I wouldn't be able to sleep at night.'

North Star Galaxy
v
Torbay Terriers

I can't prove how Sam found out, but I suspect Jack told Travis I'd paid him to play in the quarter-final, and Travis made sure the news found its way to Sam.

'I'm not playing if he's in the team!' Sam pointed a finger at me.

Doug's face darkened. 'I've had enough of this!'

I'm the manager of this team, in case you've all forgotten. So, you're both dropped!' He shook his head. 'Donut, you're in goal. Gerbil, you take Charlie's place on the right. Oscar, you're captain.'

I pulled off the armband and handed it over.

'I can't believe you paid Jack to play,' said Oscar.

'Were you gonna pay him for the semi too?' asked Gerbil.

I shrugged. I hadn't thought that far ahead. 'I just wanted Jack to play one last time to get us through the quarter-final.'

'We won the match, but what did we lose?' said Miko, and we all stared at him.

Sam was standing with Jasmine on the touchline. She stopped me before I reached them.

'I wouldn't go near Sam for a while,' she said. 'He's not talking to you, and neither am I.'

'Um . . . you just did.'

'I'm not joking, Charlie!'

I'd seen Jas angry before, but nothing like this.

'I can't believe you'd do something like that!' she said. 'And don't you DARE tell me it was for the good of the team!' She turned and stalked away.

'But it was ...' I said, too quietly to be heard.

Though I was starting to think I might have been wrong about that.

The game was a disaster. Torbay Terriers were directly below us in the league, but we made them look like Lazio in their sky-blue kit. With so many players out of position, North Star were a shambles—running into each other, and passing to people who weren't there. It might have been funny if it wasn't my team, and I didn't feel somehow responsible.

There was nothing Donut could have done about the first goal—a screamer from the edge of the box—the kind of strike TV pundits drool over.

The second went through his legs, and the third Sam would have saved with his eyes shut.

'You need to sort things out with Sam,' said Oscar at half-time.

'Or pay him,' grunted Donut.

'He won't talk to me!'

'Try putting a note through his door then,' said Nathan.

By the time the fourth goal went in, North Star had given up. Even Torbay got bored when they reached double figures. Oscar scored twice right at the end, but it was no consolation.

After the game Doug just packed up the stuff and walked towards the Hearse. Nobody said a word to me.

Thursday Night, Training

Doug took me and Sam to one side.

'It's the semi-final on Sunday,' he said. 'We'll need our strongest team against the Colts, which means you two both need to be there.'

Sam shook his head. 'I told you, I'm not playing if he's in the team.'

I thought Doug was going to explode again, but he just sighed like a deflated football and scratched his beard. 'Your choice Sam—but I'm disappointed.' He turned to me. 'You're back on the wing then, Charlie. Oscar's going to stay as captain, though. OK?'

That hurt, but I didn't blame him.

The others weren't happy when they found out about Sam.

Donut swore and folded his arms. 'I'm not going in goal!'

'They'll murder us,' said Gerbil.

Nathan just shook his head, and gave me a look that would have melted the goalposts.

IT WAS A LONG WALK HOME.

I HAD A LOT OF TIME TO THINK.

WHEN MIKO SAID WE'D LOST SOMETHING, I THOUGHT HE MEANT SAM—EVEN ME!

THEN I STARTED THINKING ABOUT THE COLTS MATCH, AND I REALIZED WE'D LOST SOMETHING MUCH MORE IMPORTANT THAN A SINGLE PLAYER.

THAT DAY WE'D PLAYED AS A TEAM—WORKING FOR EACH OTHER.

CHARLIE MERRICK'S MISFITS HAD BECOME A REAL TEAM AND I HADN'T EVEN NOTICED.

WHAT AN IDIOT!

I HAD TO PUT THINGS RIGHT—

BUT HOW?

I WAS ALMOST HOME WHEN IT FINALLY HIT ME.

DONK

Mum insisted on examining my ankle.

'It doesn't look swollen.' She prodded the joint, and I yelped for effect. Mum looked at me and frowned. 'Mmm . . . I should probably take you for an X-ray though—just in case. I'll drive you to the game afterwards if you like?'

'It's OK. I'd rather just come back here.' Watching the game would be torture knowing I should have been playing.

Mum put her arm around my shoulders. 'Whatever you want,' she said, and it was all I could do not to cry.

We'd just got in the car when a text came through from Donut to say that Sam had agreed to go in goal. I'd done what I could; the rest was up to them.

When Gerbil came round later with a match report, I was lying on the settee with a pack of frozen peas wrapped around my INJURED ANKLE.

'How's your leg?' said Gerbil.

Emily snorted. 'Three hours Mum waited at the hospital,' she said. 'They couldn't find anything wrong. I reckon they should have checked his head, not his foot!'

I ignored her. 'So, what happened in the match?'

'It was incredible!' Gerbil's face lit up. 'For five minutes we were actually winning! Oscar ran past three of 'em, then blasted it into the top corner!'

'Wow! So, what was the final score?'

'Five—three, but it was three—two for ages. We were trying so hard for an equalizer they got us twice on the counter-attack—two goals in two minutes. We got one back at the end, but it was too late.'

'How did Sam do?'

'Brilliant,' said Gerbil. 'Colts would have been three up in the first quarter of an hour if wasn't for Sam.'

I nodded, my throat too tight for words.

'You'll never guess what?' Gerbil sat down on the seat next to me. 'Doug put Miko on the wing in your position, so I went at left-back. Turns out I'm quite good in defence.' He grinned. 'Who knew!'

'That's great,' I said.

'Miko was brilliant, though,' said Gerbil. 'Dead fast. He made two, and then scored one! We should have tried him up front earlier—we could have been top of the league by now!'

I'd been right—they didn't need me.

'Anyway, I gotta go,' said Gerbil. 'I hope your ankle gets better soon.'

'Thanks.' My ankle was fine. It was the hollow ache in my chest that was causing me pain.

I thought doing the right thing was supposed to make you feel better.

It doesn't!

I needed somewhere to wallow in my misery, so I crawled upstairs for a bath. I turned on the taps and poured some bubble-bath into the water. The bottle was shaped like the World Cup, and I'll admit that once . . . or maybe three or four times, I'd posed in the bathroom mirror, holding the fake trophy, while the water roaring into the bath became a cheering crowd in my ears.

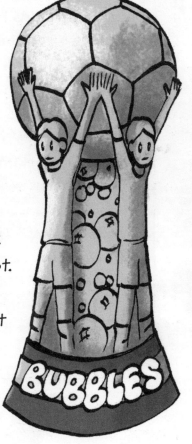

That night though, I could hardly bear to look at it. I was in such a hurry to shove the bottle back on top of the cabinet above the sink, I dropped it.

The replica World Cup plummeted like a golden brick and slammed into my right foot. There was a crunch, followed by PAIN. The kind of pain that makes you shout words you didn't realize you knew. The kind of words to bring Mum thundering up the stairs.

Twenty minutes later I was back in the Accident & Emergency department at Hardacre Hospital.

FACT

THE CURRENT WORLD CUP TROPHY WAS FIRST USED IN THE 1974 FINALS. THE ORIGINAL **JULES RIMET** WAS A STATUETTE OF **NIKE**—NOT A SOLID GOLD TRAINING SHOE, BUT THE **GREEK GODDESS OF VICTORY**. IT WAS **STOLEN TWICE**—ONCE IN 1966, WHEN IT WAS FOUND BY A DOG CALLED **PICKLES**. THE SECOND THEFT WAS IN 1984 AND THE TROPHY WAS NEVER FOUND. IT WAS PROBABLY MELTED DOWN, WHICH MEANS THAT **ALL OVER THE WORLD PEOPLE MIGHT BE WEARING JEWELLERY THAT WAS ONCE PART OF THE WORLD CUP!**

Parkview Pirates
v
North Star Galaxy

When I arrived at school on Monday, with a crutch and a ridiculous plastic sandal protecting my foot, I told everyone the BIKE ACCIDENT STORY, and didn't mention the bubble-bath. After a few days, I almost started believing the official version myself. Maybe it was less painful to accept that I had missed the semi-final through injury, rather than self-imposed exile?

The doctor told me I had badly bruised toes and something called a SUBUNGUAL HAEMATOMA. It had made the nail on my big toe go black and was responsible for the pain throbbing through my foot. She used a gigantic needle to drain the blood away, and warned me that the toenail might still fall off. She also said I wouldn't be playing football for at least a month.

MATCH REPORT SHEET

PARKVIEW PIRATES V NORTH ⭐ GALAXY

FINAL SCORE

| 4 | 2 |

HALF-TIME

| 1 | 0 |

POS	LEAGUE TABLE	PTS
9	TORBAY TERRIERS	8
10	LEIGH ROAD COSMOS	8
11	NORTH ⭐ GALAXY	8
12	HOLCOMBE WAND	7

NORTH ⭐ SQUAD

GK	SAM	
D	MOLE	
D	GERBIL	
W	MIKO	
DM	DONUT	
AM	NATHAN	
W	LUKAS	
S	OSCAR (captain)	
S	KASH	
SUB		

MATCH REPORT

Nasty match. Dunno how no one got injured or sent off! 6 yellow cards!!!!!! Back in the relegation zone too. Aggghhh!

I wanted to go and watch the game, but Mum said I had to rest my foot. I wasn't sure I'd be welcome anyway.

← Gerbil filled in the match report sheet so I could stick it in before sending this off in time for the COMPETITION DEADLINE.

I'm going to miss writing everything down. Now everyone hates me, you're the only people I can talk to! Once you've read what happened, you'll probably hate me too!

I can't believe some of the stuff I did.

I nearly took the bad parts out, so you wouldn't know. But that felt wrong. If nothing else, this is the TRUTH. That must count for something.

Charlie Merrick

(team captain)
ex

WHAT?

THAT'S IT?!

THAT CAN'T BE
THE END!

I WANT
TO KNOW
WHAT HAPPENS
NEXT.

REALLY?

OK...

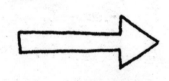

I've sent off the entry for the World Cup competition, but I decided to keep writing everything down. A story isn't over until you get to the end, and a lot could happen between now and then. There are still seven games left to save North Star from relegation, for a start!

Maybe one day someone else will read this and want to find out what happened.

So, if you're out there—whoever you are—this is for YOU!

North Star Galaxy
v
Holcombe Wanderers

Holcombe Wanderers were the only team below North Star in the league. If they beat us, we'd be back on the bottom.

Mum wrapped my comedy boot and half my leg in a black bin liner, then drove me to the park so I could watch the game.

Most of the team seemed quite pleased to see me. Sam was the only one who didn't come over. He was talking to Jasmine, and I saw them both glance in my

direction. I wondered if I should tell him I'd faked an injury just so he could play the semi-final. But given the state of my leg, he probably wouldn't believe me.

The team lined up with Miko in my place on the wing. Straight from kick-off, I saw how fast he was—more accurate with his passing than me, too. At the back, Gerbil was tackling anyone who came near him, including Donut a couple of times! You couldn't fault him for effort, though once he got the ball, it was anyone's guess where it would end up. Sam was wearing a pair of proper sports glasses, but that wasn't the only thing that seemed different about him. He looked more confident, taller perhaps.

As I watched, he dived low to his left to push away a shot heading for the bottom corner.

'How long before you're fit again Charlie?' said Doug, standing next to me on the touchline.

'Couple of weeks . . . but they look like they're doing OK without me.'

Doug raised an eyebrow. 'That doesn't sound like the Charlie Merrick I know.'

I shrugged.

'You're a good leader on the pitch, Charlie,' said Doug. 'You just need to accept you can't do everything yourself. You have to trust the people around you. That's what makes a team.' Then he dashed up the line, shouting as he went. 'Gerbil! If he's wearing a blue shirt—don't tackle him!'

'Didn't expect to see you here.' Jasmine's voice made me jump.

'I thought you weren't talking to me.'

She nodded towards my mummified foot. 'Must have been a big bottle.'

I frowned.

'Emily told me you dropped a bottle of bubble-bath on your foot,' said Jasmine. 'She also told me it happened AFTER the cup game.'

On the pitch Miko and Oscar exchanged passes and the ball flashed millimetres over the bar.

'Emily thinks you faked an injury just so Sam could play in the semi-final.' Jasmine laughed. 'I told her there was no way you would do something like that, just for a mate.'

'That would be crazy,' I said.

'All for the good of the team, eh?' said Jasmine.

I shrugged. 'Something like that.'

'You're an idiot Charlie Merrick!' Jasmine put an arm around my shoulders. 'But my kind of idiot.' Then she jumped up as Oscar was upended on the far touchline. 'That's a foul, ref!' she screamed, then turned back to me. 'By the way, I'm officially talking to you again now. Just so you know.'

North Star lost the match, and a week later got thumped by Cedar Street Wasps on their wonky pitch.

NORTH GALAXY V HOLCOMBE WANDERERS

FINAL SCORE

2	3
1	**H T**	1

POS	LEAGUE TABLE	PTS
9	HOLCOMBE WAND	10
10	TORBAY TERRIERS	8
11	LEIGH ROAD COSMOS	8
12	NORTH ☆ GALAXY	8

MATCH REPORT

We were ROBBED! No way should we have lost this game. Great goals from Oscar & Miko. Bottom of the league again now though—same points, but worse goal difference. :(

CEDAR STREET WASPS V NORTH GALAXY

FINAL SCORE

5	0
3	**H T**	0

POS	LEAGUE TABLE	PTS
9	HOLCOMBE WAND	10
10	TORBAY TERRIERS	8
11	LEIGH ROAD COSMOS	8
12	NORTH ☆ GALAXY	8

MATCH REPORT

WASPS got their revenge for us knocking them out of the cup. At least the teams just above us in the league lost too, so we're no further behind.

With the finals only a few months away, the whole country had gone World Cup mad. There were flags everywhere, flapping from cars and draped over houses; every item of food packaging had a World Cup theme. You couldn't turn on the TV or radio without some advert telling you it was time to:

SEIZE THE MOMENT

Each time I heard it, the same hollow feeling twisted my guts. I knew there was no way North Star would be chosen to play at the tournament, especially after the judges read what I'd done.

I tried to push the competition, and everything to do with the World Cup, out of my mind. I had more important things to worry about. Like the fact North Star were still BOTTOM OF THE LEAGUE.

POS		P	W	D	L	F	A	GD	PTS
8	SHUTT LANE MONARCHS	17	4	4	9	30	52	-22	16
9	HOLCOMBE WANDERERS	17	2	4	11	32	67	-35	10
10	TORBAY TERRIERS	17	1	5	11	39	71	-32	8
11	LEIGH ROAD COSMOS	17	2	2	13	28	66	-38	8
12	NORTH STAR GALAXY	17	2	2	13	18	89	-71	8

At the end of the season the last two teams would be relegated and have to re-apply to join. Other teams could vote against you—like the ones who'd complained we didn't give them a proper game—not to mention the Colts.

Relegation would mean the end of North Star Galaxy. We had to start winning some games.

Unfortunately, our next match was against Goldbridge Colts . . .

WITH FOUR GAMES TO GO AT THE END OF THE **1998-9 BUNDESLIGA** SEASON, **EINTRACHT FRANKFURT WERE SEVENTEENTH AND HEADING FOR RELEGATION.**
THEY WON THEIR NEXT THREE GAMES, BUT STILL **NEEDED TO SCORE FIVE GOALS** AGAINST DEFENDING CHAMPIONS **KAISERSLAUTERN** IN THEIR LAST MATCH. IT TOOK FRANKFURT FORTY-SEVEN MINUTES TO SCORE ONE! THEN THREE GOALS IN TWELVE MINUTES GAVE THEM HOPE. FINALLY, WITH A MINUTE TO GO, **JAN-AAGE FJÖRTOFT** SCORED A FIFTH TO GIVE FRANKFURT **ONE OF THE GREATEST ESCAPES IN THE HISTORY OF FOOTBALL!**

COULD NORTH STAR DO SOMETHING SIMILAR?

North Star Galaxy
v
Goldbridge Colts

I finally got rid of the plastic slipper and the crutch, but the doctor said it would still be a couple of weeks before I could play again. Which meant I had to watch the Colts game from the touchline.

'Didn't fancy it today then?' said Travis, even though he knew I was injured. 'You remember Jack, don't you?' He smirked, and pointed to where our former goalkeeper was warming up for the Colts.

Jasmine suggested Travis might like to depart and rejoin his teammates—though not in those exact words.

He laughed. 'Oh, did I mention the Colts are playing at the World Cup?' He waved a sheet of paper under my nose. It had a SEIZE THE MOMENT logo at the top. 'You'll be able to watch us on TV,' he said, then swaggered off across the pitch.

'Didn't you put North Star in for that?' said Jasmine.

I nodded. I'd known we wouldn't be chosen, but to have it confirmed was like a ball in the gut from close range. I felt sick.

'I think I might go home.'

Jas looked at me. 'You have gone a funny colour. D'you want me to walk you back?'

I shook my head. I needed some time alone, to feel sorry for myself.

Emily was in the kitchen.

'You're early.'

'Don't feel so good,' I said.

My sister shrugged. 'Oh, there's a letter for you.' She reached for the mountain of mail piled on top of the microwave, and for a fraction of a second hope flickered in my chest. Then Emily handed me a small blue envelope addressed in my grandma's neat handwriting.

'Is that it?'

'Why, were you expecting something?'

I sighed. 'Not really.'

It was a birthday card with footballers on. My birthday wasn't for another two weeks, but Grandma liked to make sure her cards arrived in plenty of time. I shoved the card back onto the stack of post and sent the whole lot spilling onto the floor.

'Charlie!' Emily rolled her eyes.

I crouched down to pick up the scattered mail and froze...

'When did this come?'

I didn't wait for an answer— just tore open the envelope. ⟹

SEIZE THE MOMENT

Dear Mr Merrick,

I am happy to inform you that North Star Galaxy Under-12s have been selected to participate in Fab's Football Factory World Cup Youth Tournament, at the World Cup Finals in June.

and further information and registration forms the green squad sheets

for yo

a

FAB'S FOOTBALL FACTORY

Dear Charlie,

I'm writing this note because I wanted you to know how much the judges and I enjoyed hearing about North Star Galaxy. Your drawings really brought the story to life.

We appreciated your honesty and enjoyed seeing your 'misfits' grow into a team. We are all fans of North Star now and want to know how your season ended. We hope that playing at the Wo   will be a fitting finale.

Best wishes,

Fabrice Roux

I made it back to the park just as the teams were leaving the pitch.

'Hey!' I shouted, hobbling towards the huddle of blue and yellow.

'You missed it Charlie,' said Jasmine. 'We lost!'

'I don't care about that,' I said. 'Look at this.' I handed her the letter.

Jasmine's eyes widened. 'You did it!'

'What's he done now?' said Doug, looking worried.

'Only got you a place at the World Cup!'

Suddenly everyone was crowding round to see the letter. When the scrum finally released me, I noticed Sam over by the bags, packing his stuff.

I walked across. 'So, how d'you feel about playing at the World Cup then?'

Sam shrugged, and climbed onto his bike. 'Who'd you bribe to get that?'

'What? I didn't . . .'

'Sam, there's something you should know,' said Jasmine, but he was already cycling away. 'Don't worry,' she said. 'I'll talk to him.'

I'd like to think that the World Cup news helped inspire my teammates to their first win without Jack.

Unfortunately, Torbay Terriers chose the same day to record an equally unexpected victory at Cedar Street, a result that kept us in the relegation zone.

DIRKHILL DYNAMOS V NORTH ☆ GALAXY

FINAL SCORE

2 3

1 H/T 0

POS	LEAGUE TABLE	PTS
9	HOLCOMBE WAND	14
10	TORBAY TERRIERS	11
11	NORTH ☆ GALAXY	11
12	LEIGH ROAD COSMOS	8

MATCH REPORT

WE WON! Our first league win in nine games! We were behind twice, but Oscar's hat-trick gave us 3 goals and 3 points—enough to lift North ☆ off the bottom!

When I completed a full training session four days later, Doug said I'd be in the squad for Sunday. I thought Sam might complain, but he didn't say anything.

North Star Galaxy
v
Shutt Lane Monarchs

I always get nervous before a match, but that day was worse than usual. Since I'd last played, North Star had grown into a proper team, and I couldn't help thinking that they didn't need me any more. Which must have been how Sam felt when Jack arrived.

When Shutt Lane scored, I was almost relieved. I didn't want us to lose—it just made me feel like I might be some use after all.

A minute later we equalized.

Then, just before half-time, Oscar weaved his way into the Monarchs' penalty box and slid the ball past the keeper to put us into the lead.

When Kash hobbled off ten minutes into the second half, Doug put me on with strict instructions to PLAY SAFE and defend the lead. 'Don't go haring off trying to score,' he said. 'Keep it tight!'

I did my best, but a month off had left me slow and clumsy. I kept giving away fouls, and my passes were either too short, or wildly over hit. I saw Doug talking to Kash, and had the feeling I wouldn't be on the pitch much longer.

Then a clearance from Gerbil looped over my head and bounced in front of me.

Shutt Lane had just taken a corner. Their entire team had gone up, leaving just one defender between me and the goal.

What was I supposed to do?

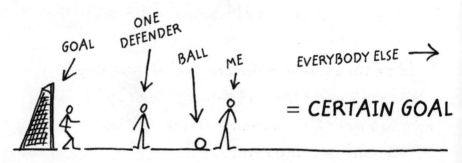

GOAL   ONE DEFENDER   BALL   ME   EVERYBODY ELSE →

= CERTAIN GOAL

I just wanted to justify my place in the team.
Another goal would have sealed it for us. All I had
to do was beat one defender...

I crossed the halfway line, and he moved towards
me—small and skinny, his shirt hanging like a dress
over his shorts. One burst of speed and I'd be past
him and through on goal.

OR...

I'd be face down in the grass, while the tiny
Monarch slipped the ball through the gap I had
left, to where his teammates were waiting.
You can guess the rest...

LEAGUE POSITIONS
2 GAMES REMAINING

		PTS
8	SHUTT LANE	17
9	HOLCOMBE	15
10	TORBAY	14
11	NORTH STAR	12
12	LEIGH ROAD	8

FULL-TIME

NORTH STAR 2-2 MONARCHS

UPCOMING FIXTURES

(11th) NORTH STAR V LEIGH ROAD (12th)
(10th) TORBAY V DIRKHILL (7th)

THE BOTTOM THREE TEAMS ARE ALL IN DANGER OF
RELEGATION, BUT ONLY ONE CAN SURVIVE. THE NEXT TWO
MATCHES WILL DECIDE WHO STAYS, AND WHO GOES!

'Well done lads,' said Doug. 'That's two unbeaten now!'

'We could have won if someone hadn't gone for
glory,' muttered Sam.

I knew he was right, but I still turned on him.
'Yeah? Well, I reckon a half-decent keeper would
have saved it!'

Sam leapt at me, fists flying. We landed in a heap and rolled round for a few seconds, before Doug and Molly pulled us apart.

'Right! That's it!' Doug pointed a trembling finger at us. 'I've had enough of you two. Last warning. Get it sorted or you're BOTH dropped! And that includes the WORLD CUP!'

STATMAN ☆ FACT

THE AWARD FOR **BIGGEST ON-PITCH PUNCH-UP** GOES TO **SPORTIVO AMELIANO** AND **GENERAL CABALLERO** IN PORTUGAL. THE FIGHT STARTED OVER A DISPUTED RED CARD AND ENDED TEN MINUTES LATER WHEN THE REF **SENT OFF A TOTAL OF EIGHTEEN PLAYERS!**

Leigh Road Cosmos
v
North Star Galaxy

After giving Sam a day to cool off, Jasmine persuaded me to bike round to his house. But when I got there, Sam wouldn't answer the door. For as long as I could remember, the three of us had spent every half-term hanging out together, and it felt weird without him.

On Wednesday evening Jasmine phoned to say she was bored, and invited me to her house. It had to be better than moping around on my own.

'Charlie!' Jasmine's mum wrapped me in a hug. 'So glad you could come to our Pamper Party!'

'Your what?'

'Pamper Party,' said Jas, appearing behind her.

'We've got massage in the bedrooms, facials in the bathroom, pedicure in the dining room, and manicure in the lounge.' She steered me along the hallway. 'Or, if you don't like the look of this, you could go and hide in the garage with my dad and Sam.'

'Sam?'

'Your choice Charlie. Stay here with us girls, or go and talk to Sam.'

'This is a set-up!' I said.

'Finally, he gets it!' Jasmine frowned. 'I tried leaving you to sort it out, and look what happened.'

We'd arrived in the kitchen. A woman with an orange face smiled up at me. 'Hello there! Would sir like to try some of our male grooming products?'

I bolted for the garage.

Sam looked shocked when I walked in. I guessed Jasmine had tricked him into coming too.

'Decided to hide out with the boys then!' Jasmine's dad grinned, and handed me a pool cue. 'You're just in time. Sam's just slaughtered me. I need some sustenance from the kitchen. You two fellas want anything?'

'I should probably get going, actually,' said Sam, placing his cue on the table.

Jasmine's dad shrugged. 'Sure thing. Just hang on while I get Jas.'

He closed the door and the silence boomed around us. Sam turned his back and started re-setting the pool table.

Did Jas really think this was going to work? Maybe it had to. There was no way I was missing the chance to play at the World Cup, and I didn't want Sam to miss out either.

'I'm sorry . . . about Sunday,' I said.

Sam didn't answer.

'It was my fault. You're a great keeper. Nobody

could have saved that shot.'

'I don't actually care what you think,' said Sam.

I sighed. 'Look. Can't we just forget about everything that's happened and . . . I don't know . . . start again?'

Sam snorted. 'You want me to FORGET that my SO-CALLED best friend deliberately lied to me? Maybe if someone had done that to YOU, you'd realize it's not so easy to forgive and forget.'

He walked round the table towards the door. 'Don't worry, I've told Doug we've sorted everything out, so you don't need to stress about missing the World Cup. But you're mad if you think we can be mates again.'

Sam reached the door and pulled the handle. 'It's locked!'

'Are you sure?' I tried it myself. 'I'll phone Jas,' I said, then realized I'd left my mobile at home.

Sam grunted and walked back to the pool table.

'Want a game while we wait?' I said.

'No,' said Sam.

Five minutes later, Jasmine's face appeared at the door.

'It's locked,' I shouted through the glass.

'I know! I locked it.'

Sam appeared next to me. 'Open the door Jas, I want to go home.'

Jasmine shook her head. 'I'll let you out when you two are friends again.'

'Are you serious?' said Sam.

'Oh, yes.'

'But that's . . . kidnapping!' I pointed out.

'Actually, it's not,' said Jasmine. 'I spoke to both your families. They're fed up with the two of you moping around. They said I should keep you here until you both see sense.'

'Not gonna happen,' said Sam.

'There's a selection of snacks and drinks in the cupboard, and you know where the toilet is.'

'Have you gone mad?!' I said.

'No! You and Sam not being friends any more—that's MAD.' Jasmine raised her eyebrows, then walked back into the house.

8:37 P.M.

'Do you really think they'll keep us here all night?'

'There's two sleeping bags and blankets behind the sofa,' said Sam. 'And it's not like we've got to go to school now it's half-term.'

I opened a bag of crisps. 'I say we give it an hour, then tell them we're best friends again and they'll let us out.'

'Or ...' said Sam. 'We call their bluff. Let's stay here. See who cracks first. They can't force us to be friends.' He scowled towards the locked door.

'I like your style!' I said.

Sam grunted.

10:07 P.M.

While Sam took out his frustration on the pool table, I switched on the games console and loaded Pro Soccer.

'Hey, d'you remember that summer we tried to play every game in the World Cup on Pro?'

Sam grunted.

'Full ninety-minute games! What was the score in that match? Algeria versus Slovenia . . . twenty-three—nineteen!'

'It was twenty-three—fifteen, actually.'

'Then my telly overheated and we couldn't finish the game!'

Sam looked up, then frowned towards the door. When I turned round, I saw Jasmine peering in at us.

'Remember,' he muttered. 'Call their bluff.'

'This is a waste of time,' I shouted through the glass. 'You can keep us locked in here for the rest of our lives. It won't change anything.'

Sam pushed past me and thumped the door with

his fist. 'I'm warning you, Jas! If I have to spend the night in here with HIM—you're going to be cleaning up a crime scene in the morning!'

Jasmine frowned and shook her head. 'Suit yourselves! I'm going to bed.'

Sam watched her go, then shrugged. 'Early days,' he said.

'What you said about a crime scene . . . you were joking, right?'

He didn't answer.

EXHIBIT A:
SOME CRISPS
(SMOKY BACON
FLAVOUR).

EXHIBIT B:
SPECTACLES
(COULD BELONG
TO MURDERER).

EXHIBIT C:
POOL CUE
(BLOODSTAINED)

8:19 A.M.

Next morning, Jasmine's dad brought breakfast. He sat down and started going on about all the friends he'd lost contact with, and how much he regretted it. Me and Sam glared at each other until he gave up and stomped off to work in a bad mood.

'Think we won that round,' said Sam, when he'd gone.

Three hours later we were still locked in the garage.

'Is Pro Soccer still loaded?' Sam picked up a controller. 'I feel like giving someone a good pasting.'

'That's fighting talk,' I said.

He snorted, but I saw a smile twitch the corners of his mouth.

6:23 P.M.

We were playing Pro Soccer when Jasmine finally unlocked the door.

'I give up,' she said. 'If you two don't want to be friends, that's your loss. You're free to go.'

'We just need to finish this tournament,' I told her.
'Next game's the final.'

'Give us half an hour,' said Sam.

When Jas slammed the door, Sam and I grinned
and gave each other a high-five—which is when the
camera flashed.

'Ha!' said Jasmine. 'Got you!'

But, for the first time in ages, I really didn't mind
losing. In fact, it felt kind of great.

MATCH REPORT SHEET

LEIGH ROAD COSMOS V NORTH ⭐ GALAXY

FINAL SCORE
1	1

HALF-TIME
1	0

POS	LEAGUE TABLE	PTS
9	HOLCOMBE WAND	16
10	TORBAY TERRIERS	15
11	NORTH ⭐ GALAXY	13
R	LEIGH ROAD COSMOS	9

MATCH REPORT

Miko's late equalizer put COSMOS down and gave us a chance. Torbay only drew with Dirkhill so **we could still survive if we beat them next week!** No pressure, then!

NORTH ⭐ SQUAD

GK	SAM	
D	MOLE	
D	DONUT	
D	GERBIL	
W	CHARLIE	
M	NATHAN	
W	KASH	
S	OSCAR (captain)	
S	MIKO	⚽
SUB	LUKAS	

Torbay Terriers
v
North Star Galaxy

AFTER THE BLOOD, SWEAT, AND TEARS OF A LONG SEASON, IT ALL COMES DOWN TO THIS: ONE GAME. ONE WINNER. ONE LOSER. SURVIVAL OR RELEGATION!

A DRAW WILL BE ENOUGH FOR TORBAY. NORTH STAR MUST WIN!

Torbay Terriers lined up with two defensive banks between us and the goal. It was like trying to play football through a forest of densely packed trees. There were sky-blue shirts everywhere. I was so sure they had extra players on the pitch, I counted twice to check.

Moments after kick-off it started to rain, icy needles soaking through our shirts and churning the pitch to treacle. For half an hour we toiled through the mud, then squelched off with the scores still level.

'How are we supposed to score if we can't get near their goal?' said Kash, picking clumps of mud from his socks.

'Just keep getting those balls up to Miko and Oscar,' said Doug. 'You'll get a chance.'

'We'd better,' said Oscar. 'If North Star get relegated I'd have to play for Colts, and that's NEVER gonna happen!'

That was all the motivation we needed.

But the goal still wouldn't come.

AT THE MOMENT NORTH STAR LOOK LIKE A TEAM ...

... WHO COULDN'T BUY A GOAL IN A GOAL SHOP WITH A FREE GOAL VOUCHER!

Every time the ball made it through to Oscar or Miko, they disappeared in a sky-blue swarm. We needed a different approach.

As Gerbil prepared to take a throw-in, I ran over to Nathan.

'Next time you get the ball,' I said, 'I'll make a run and start calling for it. Wait as long as you can . . . until someone moves away from Miko to mark me, then give it to Miko.'

Nathan frowned. 'You think that'll work?'

'Only one way to find out.'

A minute later we did.

Unfortunately, the Torbay defenders guessed I was a decoy and stayed tight on Miko. I was as surprised as them when Nathan actually passed the ball to ME.

Before I had time to think—or panic—I turned and shot.

To my surprise, the ball didn't spin off towards the corner flag—it flew past the keeper, smacked against the post and dribbled across the goalmouth.

For a second nobody moved . . .

Then, like a pack of dogs on a discarded beefburger . . . we pounced.

I'm not sure whose boot made the connection that sent the ball spinning into the back of the net. It didn't matter. At last—WE'D SCORED!

Suddenly Torbay weren't so focused on defence. We held on until the fifty-third minute, when a scuffed shot hit Donut's knee and wrong-footed Sam.

'Come on, North Star!' I clapped my hands. 'We only need one goal. There's still time!' Though how much, I wasn't sure.

It was still raining. Both teams were so plastered in mud it was hard to tell one from the other.

As we mounted a final desperate attack, the Terriers' centre back slipped, and Oscar was through. He skidded past the first challenge, dodged a second, then chipped the ball over the on-rushing goalkeeper into the net.

I opened my mouth to cheer, then stopped.

Oscar and the Torbay keeper had collided and were lying in a tangled heap. The goalie got to his feet, but Oscar stayed down, clutching his knee and writhing in the mud. When the adults ran onto the pitch, we knew something was seriously wrong. Then Nathan's dad and one of the Torbay parents lifted Oscar and carried him off to the changing hut.

Doug gathered us together. 'Oscar's going to be OK, but he injured himself scoring that goal. Don't let it be for nothing!'

When Terriers won a corner, the ref had already looked at his watch twice. On the touchline Doug was hopping from one foot to another, pointing at his wrist. This HAD to be last kick of the game.

'Just get rid of it lads!' Sam shouted, as we jostled in the area waiting for the cross to come in.

But Torbay took it short. Half our team raced out to tackle—which was exactly what they wanted. The previously crowded box was wide open. As the ball dropped into the space, the Terriers number seven volleyed it goalwards.

I'm not sure what happened next. Nobody was filming, so I guess we'll never know exactly how Sam managed to tip that shot over the bar. It was probably the greatest save I've ever seen—or rather, blinked and missed.

Seconds later, the referee blew his whistle.

We yelled. We danced. We jumped on top of Sam.

Then we went to tell Oscar we'd DONE IT! That

NORTH STAR WERE SAFE!

Which is when I realized something important. Sometimes, finishing one place above the relegation zone feels just as good as winning the league. Who would have guessed that?

FINAL LEAGUE TABLE

POS		P	W	D	L	F	A	GD	PTS
1	GOLDBRIDGE COLTS	22	22	0	0	153	31	122	66
2	FIVE ACRE	22	15	5	2	87	35	52	50
3	MAYFIELD BOROUGH	22	15	5	2	73	39	34	50
4	CEDAR STREET WASPS	22	13	5	4	88	38	50	44
5	WESTON ROAD MAGPIES	22	8	6	8	66	57	9	30
6	PARKVIEW PIRATES	22	7	6	9	51	63	-12	27
7	DIRKHILL DYNAMOS	22	7	5	10	51	60	-9	26
8	SHUTT LANE MONARCHS	22	4	6	12	35	75	-40	18
9	HOLCOMBE WANDERERS	22	3	8	11	43	77	-34	17
10	NORTH STAR GALAXY	22	4	4	14	28	103	-75	16
11	TORBAY TERRIERS	22	3	6	13	48	84	-36	15
12	LEIGH ROAD COSMOS	22	2	3	17	32	84	-52	9

to settle in Cup clash!

Local rivals go head to head

Two rival football teams from the Hardacre & District under-12s league have been chosen for the pre-match tournament at this year's World Cup. What's more, they've been drawn to play each other!

From the thousands who applied, just 112 teams were selected in four age-group categories to compete in four knock-out competitions. This means only one of our local hopefuls will make it through to the next round. Games will be played before each group and knock-out stage of the World Cup, with the finals being held before the World Cup final itself!

The matches are billed as a warm-up to the main event, but for the players involved, these will be the biggest games of their lives. Herald reporter Tony Fletcher met the teams for some friendly pre-match banter.

"We've already beaten North Star three times this season, so getting through round one won't be a problem for us!" said Colts' captain, Travis Johnson. His team are full of confidence, having won both the District Cup and promotion to Division One in their first season!

Two miles away in Northfield Park, local rivals North Star Galaxy have had a more difficult time. An injury to striker Oscar Watts means they will be without their star player for the World Cup. "Oscar scored almost all our goals this season, including the one that saved us from relegation,' explained captain Charlie Merrick. "We want to win this match for him."

Adding extra spice to the contest is the fact that Colts have many ex-Galaxy players in their squad, including goalkeeper Jack Doyle, a former United academy student.

It's sure to be a great occasion, and the Herald wishes both teams the best of luck.

I NEED THE TOILET...

WHOSE BRILLIANT IDEA WAS THIS ANYWAY?

CHARLIE!!!

to lower league

WORLD CUP PRE-MATCH TOURNAMENT:

North Star Galaxy
v
Goldbridge Colts

It was six hours until kick-off in the World Cup Group B match between France and Mexico, but there were already people outside the stadium in coloured wigs and face paint, with flags draped around their shoulders like capes. Huge SEIZE THE MOMENT billboards loomed over us as the coach turned into the car park.

A woman in a dark-blue suit came out to meet us. 'You must be North Star Galaxy,' she said. 'My name's Sarah. I'll be looking after you today.'

We followed her through a door into a narrow blue and white corridor.

'The French and Mexican teams are in the new dressing rooms in the main stand,' she said, 'but

these are the ones we've been using all season.' She
led us into a vast blue room with wooden lockers and
benches along the walls. There was a table in the
centre, stacked with fresh fruit and energy drinks.

'Wow!' Gerbil's mouth hung open.

'This is bigger than my house!' said Oscar, clacking
across the tiled floor on his crutches.

Sarah smiled. 'You get the home dressing room.
It's much larger than the one your opponents
are in, but don't tell them!'

'For once we get a better deal than the
Colts!' said Sam.

I hung my shirt above the bench and sat down.

Opposite me, Sam was doing the same thing—his red, lucky thirteen keeper's top swinging from a peg.

'It's just a dream,' he said, grinning. 'We'll wake up in a minute!'

We got changed and Doug wrote the team on a flipchart with pre-printed pitch markings.

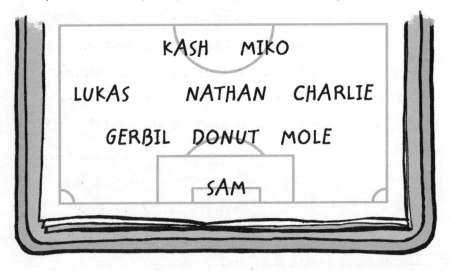

KASH   MIKO

LUKAS   NATHAN   CHARLIE

GERBIL DONUT MOLE

SAM

A few minutes later the referee came in. He introduced himself and went through the tournament rules.

'I'll ring the buzzer five minutes before I need you lined up in the corridor, ready to go,' he said. 'Now,

don't forget, lads—enjoy it! This is the World Cup!'
He smiled and left.

'Did he have to remind us?' said Donut, clutching
his stomach and heading for the toilet.

I looked at the collection of misfits in the room—
substitutes and no hopers, the wrong size or the
wrong shape. Mole, picking a scab on his knee; Gerbil,
looking around the room and grinning like an idiot;
Donut (just back from the toilet), pale and scared;
Lukas, eyes closed, headphones in; Nathan, slowly
rotating his neck like a boxer preparing for a fight;
Kash, fiddling with his hair and chewing wildly; Miko,
head bowed, rolling a ball beneath his foot. And Sam,
my best friend in the whole world, looking calmer
than any of us, wiping his glasses on his shirt and
smiling at me.

The buzzer made me jump.

'Five minutes, boys,' said Doug, clapping his hands.
'Gather round!' He unfolded a sheet of paper from
his pocket.

'Don't tell me he's written a speech!' Sam groaned.

'Six-one,' read
Doug. 'Four—nil.
Five—nil. Nine—one.'
'Is this supposed to help?' said Sam.
'Eleven—nil. Seven—two.' Doug
paused. 'At the start of the season,
we were a joke. Now look at you.
You've earned the right to be here
today, don't forget that! Colts might
have won the league and the cup,
but you've achieved so much more—
you've become a TEAM. Results ...'
He screwed the piece of paper
into a ball and tossed it
over his head.

'It's the team that matters. Right, Charlie?'
'Right,' I said.

It was a long walk to the double doors marked
PITCH. Sarah had explained that the dressing rooms
were soundproofed, but in the corridor you could
hear the crowd like a storm approaching.

'I need the toilet!' said Donut.

'No you don't,' said Doug.

The referee and his assistants were waiting. So
were the Colts, lined up in matching gold tracksuits.

My mouth felt like I'd been gargling glue. All the
times I'd dreamt about this, I'd never imagined my
knees would shake so much I wouldn't be able to
walk, let alone kick a football. But this was a dream
come true . . .

Or a nightmare I couldn't wake up from!

'Ready, lads?' The referee didn't wait for an
answer, just turned and pushed open the doors.

Noise rushed in like water through a burst dam. Horns blared, drums thumped so loud they rattled my teeth. We walked out into a white canvas tunnel and a cool breeze shivered round my legs. Then the music dipped and the stadium announcer's voice boomed over the speakers.

'And NOW, the final first-round game of our under-12s tournament. Please WELCOME ONTO THE FIELD—Goldbridge COLTS—and NORTH—STAR—GALAXEEE!'

'Charlie! Move!' Sam nudged me in the back, and I willed my jelly legs into action.

The pitch felt endless, impossibly smooth and green.

'Beats the park,' said Sam.

Gerbil laughed. 'I bet they don't have to mine-sweep this place before kick-off!'

I gazed up at the stands towering over us, and saw thousands of faces staring back at me. Amongst the green sombreros and multi-coloured masks of the Mexican fans, and the red, white and blue of France, I saw the yellow of Brazil; the pale blue and white of

Argentina; flags from South Africa, USA, Germany, Nigeria...

Then the referee was calling me and Travis into the centre.

We shook hands and I called tails as the coin spun in the air.

'Tails it is,' said the ref.

'Well, at least you won something today,' said Travis.

And then Miko and Kash were standing next to me in the centre circle. I glanced over my shoulder and Sam gave a thumbs up. Then the whistle blew, and we were off...

FACT

THE BIGGEST CROWD FOR A WORLD CUP FINALS MATCH WAS AT THE **ESTÁDIO DO MARACANÃ** IN RIO DE JANEIRO IN 1950, WHEN **173,850 PEOPLE** WATCHED **URUGUAY** BEAT **BRAZIL** 2–1. DURING THE FIRST WORLD CUP FINALS IN 1930, A MERE **300 FANS** SAW **ROMANIA** ROMP HOME 3–1, WINNERS OVER PERU—THE SMALLEST CROWD EVER!

HALF-TIME
COLTS   3
NORTH STAR   0

'You're doing great, lads!' said Doug, handing out bottles of water.

'We're three—nil down!' Donut's voice honked through his bandaged nose.

'Liverpool were three—nil down at half-time in Istanbul,' said Kash. 'They still won.'

Nathan snorted. 'Liverpool were never this bad!'

'I wish Oscar was playing,' said Gerbil.

'So do I!' Oscar was sweating from the effort of hobbling onto the pitch. He waved a crutch at us. 'It's torture watching you lot!'

Suddenly everyone seemed really interested in their boots.

'You're treating the Colts like they're something

special,' said Oscar. 'They're just rich kids with hair gel!' He shook his head. 'You don't need me . . . or Jack. North Star is a team now, you idiots!'

'Oscar's right,' I said. 'I thought we needed a star player to save us—and look what happened! Don't forget, we're not just called North Star . . . we're North Star GALAXY! And a galaxy is made up of billions of stars, not just one!'

'So . . . who wants to stick it to the Colts for Oscar?' said Sam.

Which is probably what I should have said.

Two minutes into the second half we won a corner.
Jack was first to it, but under pressure from Nathan
he could only punch clear. The ball landed at
Donut's feet.

For a second Donut looked like he might faint, then he kicked it away as fast as possible. The ball zoomed back into the crowded penalty area, pinballed off three players, and flew past a startled Jack into the net.

Donut looked almost as surprised as the Colts.

Not used to being under attack, the Colts started to make mistakes. Nathan intercepted a weak pass on the halfway line and knocked it wide to me.

I headed for the touchline, and as the Colt defender moved in to tackle, switched the ball inside to Miko. Our substitute striker swerved past one challenge, beat the second with a burst of speed, then curled a low shot towards the bottom corner. It was perfect, but I'd forgotten about Jack.

An octopus limb unfurled
   . . . and tipped the ball
      . . . onto the post . . .

and into the net! On the touchline, Oscar threw his crutches into the air and fell over.

NORTH STAR HAVE TURNED THIS GAME AROUND!

BUT CAN THEY GET A THIRD?

The only downside of scoring goals is that it makes the other team angry.

For the next five minutes the ball didn't leave our half. We blocked, we tackled, and if one white shirt was beaten, another appeared in its place.

Then Colts were awarded a PENALTY!

Gerbil said it was a dive, but the referee wasn't listening.

The giant screen displayed less than five minutes to go.

I couldn't watch.

When the crowd cheered I didn't know what it meant, until I opened my eyes and saw Sam disappear under a pile of blue and yellow bodies. He'd saved it!

Colts were still arguing and blaming each other when Sam booted the ball out. I realized I was the only North Star player in the Colts half and started to run. If I let the ball bounce, the defenders chasing after me would catch up. My only chance was to try to head it first time. This was going to hurt!

KEEP YOUR EYE ON THE BALL, CHARLIE.

AIM FOR A GOOD CLEAN CONNECTION WITH YOUR FOREHEAD.

FR

As the ball dropped from the sky like a pale meteor, I closed my eyes. Seconds later something hard whacked into the top of my head and knocked me over. Through the blinding pain I was vaguely aware the crowd were cheering . . . or maybe it was the sound of thirty-thousand people laughing?

When I dared open my eyes, the first thing I saw was the replay on the big screen. It showed a boy who looked remarkably like me, heading the ball over Jack into the goal.

I'D SCORED!

A HEADER!!

We were LEVEL!!!

ANOTHER GOAL AND WE'D WIN!!!!

Was this possible? Or had I been knocked unconscious? But the pain in my head felt too real to be part of a dream.

Moments later, Gerbil won the ball and banged it up to Kash. Our number twenty-three sprinted towards the corner flag then sent a cross into the area. Miko darted through a swarm of white shirts and volleyed it goalwards. Nobody except Jack could have saved it.

As our ex-goalkeeper cleared the ball downfield, the referee glanced at his watch.

'HANDBALL!' It was so blatant, Sam was laughing. He stopped when the referee shook his head. 'HE PUNCHED IT!' shouted Sam. 'How could you not see that?'

But the referee turned and ran back towards the centre, leaving us to stare at each other in disbelief.

Seconds after we kicked off the final whistle sounded.

Around me, players in blue and yellow sank to the ground, heads buried in their hands.

Doug appeared on the pitch. There were tears in his eyes, but he was smiling! I didn't understand, until Sam grabbed me.

'Can you hear that?'

He pointed towards the stands, and I saw the entire crowd were on their feet. They were chanting too, but it wasn't Goldbridge Colts' name echoing around the stadium—it was NORTH STAR!

As captain, it was my job to lead the team onto the podium to receive our commemorative medals. My chest was bursting with the injustice of what had happened, and with the chants of the crowd still buzzing in my ears, I wasn't really concentrating. I didn't notice who was waiting on the platform with a medal draped over his hand, until I looked up.

'FABRICE ROUX!' My voice came out in a squeak.

'Charlie Merrick!' Fabrice Roux grinned his famous grin and shook my hand. 'It is good to finally meet you! I feel like I know everyone already—from your drawings!' He hung the medal round my neck. 'Well played today, Charlie. A good header. Especially with your eyes closed!' Fabrice winked, then turned to Sam.

I walked down the steps in a daze, and Doug grabbed my arm. 'Charlie! Fabrice Roux just invited us to his academy in France! He's running a summer training camp, with teams from all over the world!'

'What?' I stared at him, then sighed. 'I suppose he invited the Colts too?'

'No, just us!'

My mouth opened, but the part of my brain controlling speech seemed to have shut down from shock. It helped dull the pain of having to clap while Goldbridge collected their winners' medals.

'They'd better get knocked out in the next round,' said Sam, folding his arms.

Then Fabrice stepped to the front of the platform and spoke into a microphone. 'Now, it is my great pleasure to present today's award for Man-of-the-Match.' He held up a small gold trophy.

Sam growled. 'If it's Travis, you'd better hold me back!'

'It is often a difficult task to single out just one player,' said Fab. 'Today it was impossible. So, we are doing something different. We are giving the Man-of-the-Match award . . . to a whole team!'

Applause rippled across the stands.

'Out on the pitch today, these young footballers showed us ALL how to play as a team.' He paused.

'And that team is . . . NORTH STAR GALAXY!'

The crowd erupted.

We stared at him.

'But we lost!' said Donut.

Fabrice grinned. 'Sometimes the best team does lose,' he whispered, holding the trophy towards us.

'Take it then!' hissed Sam, digging me in the ribs.

The cup felt cold and heavy in my hands. When I lifted it above my head, the image was displayed on the big screen. The crowd leapt to their feet, and once more the name of North Star Galaxy rang out across the stadium.

There were lots of photos taken that day, but this one is my favourite. Jas took it from the stand, which is why it's a bit wonky. I like it because it looks like us—my team of misfits—the best team in the world!

(back row) Fabrice Roux! Doug, Oscar, Donut, Lukas, Gerbil, Nathan, (front) Mole, Kash, Miko, Sam, Me!

For now . . .

NORTH STAR GALAXY

NICKNAME
Misfits

FORMED
1985

HONOURS
Div. 2 Champions 1989
Div. 2 Champions 1992
Cup Winners 1999
Div. 2 Champions 2010

GROUND

NORTHFIELD PARK

HOME KIT

AWAY KIT

Collector's Album: NORTH STAR GALAXY

MANAGER

DOUG

NAME: DONUT'S DAD
SKILLS: Mad enough to manage us. Can't see how bad we are!
NOT SO GOOD AT: Tactics.
⭐ **FACT:** If you turn his head upside down he looks like Dennis the Menace! **TRY IT**

GOALKEEPER

13

SAM

NAME: SAMSON CHARSLEY
(seriously! His mum's a bit weird.)
SKILLS: Has no fear!
NOT SO GOOD AT: Corners and high shots. Very small for a goalie.
⭐ **FACT:** Sleeps in his lucky No.13 shirt the night before every match.

GOALKEEPER

1

JACK

NAME: JACK DOYLE
SKILLS: Awesome goalkeeping.
NOT SO GOOD AT: Shooting. (Secretly, he wants to be a striker.)
⭐ **FACT:** Used to play for a famous Premiership team's Youth Academy.

DEFENDER

4

MOLE

NAME: EOIN MOLES
SKILLS: Good tackler.
NOT SO GOOD AT: Ball control. Once he has won the ball, Mole usually gives it away again!
⭐ **FACT:** Wears his shorts back to front for good luck.

Collector's Album: NORTH STAR GALAXY

MIDFIELDER

6

DONUT

NAME: DUNCAN DEVEY
(Duncan Donut! Get it??!!)
SKILLS: Can kick and head the
ball further than anyone else.
NOT SO GOOD AT: Running, passing.
⭐ **FACT:** Donut doesn't eat donuts.
He doesn't like cakes at all!

MIDFIELDER

5

NATHAN

NAME: NATHAN SHORT
SKILLS: Scares the opposition.
NOT SO GOOD AT: Staying on the
pitch. Gets lots of cards.
⭐ **FACT:** No nickname. Nathan
likes to be called NATHAN.
Don't argue. Seriously. Don't.

WINGER

7

CHARLIE

NAME: CHARLIE MERRICK
SKILLS: Never gives up. Good
leader on the pitch. (I'm not
being big-headed, that's what
our manager, Doug, said!)
NOT SO GOOD AT: Heading, shooting.
⭐ **FACT:** Team Captain.

WINGER

23

KASH

NAME: KASHIF KHAN
SKILLS: Fast, but sometimes
forgets to take the ball with him.
NOT SO GOOD AT: Headers, too
worried about messing up his hair.
⭐ **FACT:** Wears No.23 in honour
of his hero David Beckham.

Collector's Album: NORTH STAR GALAXY

STRIKER

10

OSCAR

NAME: OSCAR WATTS
SKILLS: Lots! Best player in team.
NOT SO GOOD AT: Not getting fouled—gets injured a lot.
⭐ **FACT:** Youngest person to win Hardacre Holidaze Holiday Camp 'keepy-uppy' contest, aged 6.

STRIKER

9

LUKAS

NAME: LUKAS KRYSIAK
SKILLS: Strong and fearless.
NOT SO GOOD AT: Dribbling, passing, shooting, tackling.
⭐ **FACT:** Has played in every position on the pitch, but is still trying to find the right one.

STRIKER

8

MIKO

NAME: MIKOTO SUZUKI
SKILLS: Speed. Shooting.
NOT SO GOOD AT: Tackling.
⭐ **FACT:** Miko doesn't say much. In fact, some of the team claim they don't know what his voice sounds like!

SUPER-SUB

12

GERBIL

NAME: CIARAN MORGAN
SKILLS: Never stops smiling.
NOT SO GOOD AT: Football.
⭐ **FACT:** Gerbil has never scored a goal, even in training. When he misses Gerb shrugs & says 'one day'. That day is yet to arrive . . .

PLAYER PR★FILE

WRITER

8

DAVE

NAME: DAVE COUSINS
SKILLS: Scribbling & doodles.
NOT SO GOOD AT: Spelling.
★ **FACT:** Despite limited ability at full-sized football, Dave is a demon at SUBBUTEO*. His two-handed corners are legendary.

POSITION: Writer/Illustrator. (current position: in the attic!)
FOOTBALL POSITION: Goalkeeper; Right-back.
PLAYING CAREER: Raunds Tigers U-13s (1981-2).
FAVOURITE TEAM: Birmingham City.

Dave Cousins' football career was cut short— literally—when the goals got bigger, but Dave didn't! He had a brief spell as right-back for Raunds Tigers under-13s, but could never reproduce on the field the skills he imagined in his head, or drew in his comics.

Dave's first published story was in a Birmingham City matchday programme! *The Floodlight Man*, a story about going to his first match, aged 7, was also broadcast on Radio Five Live, read by Dave himself.

As well as *Charlie Merrick's Misfits*, Dave has published two novels for teenagers: the award-winning *15 Days Without a Head*, and *Waiting for Gonzo*, which was nominated for the Carnegie Medal.

Find out more at **www.davecousins.net**.

---

* SUBBUTEO Table Soccer: the best indoor football game in the world—EVER!
(Subbuteo © Hasbro)

"A galaxy is made up of billions of stars, not just one!"

Thank you to . . .

Club President: Liz Cross
Director: Jasmine Richards
First Team Manager: Clare Whitston
Assistant Manager:
Claire Westwood
First Team Coach: Molly Dallas
Development Squad: Sarah Manson
Goalkeeping Coach: Jane Cousins
Academy Manager: Dylan Cousins
(thanks for the advice, interview
Qs, and extra artwork.)
Chief Scouts: Ptolemy Spare,
Hockley Spare
Director of Football: Mike Cousins
(thanks for all the books, advice,
and for sharing the long road of
joys and sorrow. KRO!)
Kit Man: Garrie Fletcher (thanks
for Holcombe Wanderers, and for
hours of company on the terraces
and Subbuteo pitch!)
Club Doctor: Joanna Cannon
Medical Team: Harriet Bayly,
Charlotte Armstrong, Helen Bray
Head of Football Administration:
Elaine McQuade
Physiotherapy: Louise Brown and her
team at OUP

Performance Analysts: Tracey Turner
and Beth Cox
Overseas Scouts: Anne-Marie Hansen,
Valentina Fazio, Giuseppe Trapani,
Ellena Johnstone, and all the Rights
Team at OUP
Matchday Stewards: Tony and Viv
Martin, Steve and Josie Martin,
David Hughes, Chris Griffin, Phil
Tayler
The Original Torbay Terriers:
Ma 'n' Pa Raven
Floodlight Man: Richard De'Ath
(thanks for lighting the way, Rich!)

Special thanks to Oscar Durrant for
allowing me to use his name, and
skills, in this story.

Finally, to everyone who showed
me the right way to hold a pencil
over the years—Mavis Davies, Pam
Cousins, John Hargreaves, Liz
Payne, and all my art
teachers—this is your fault!

FANZ★NE!
with JASMINE LAWRENCE

TODAY ON FAN ZONE—AN INTERVIEW WITH AUTHOR/ILLUSTRATOR DAVE COUSINS.

FIRST THINGS FIRST, OTHER THAN NORTH STAR, WHO DO YOU SUPPORT?

BIRMINGHAM CITY. MY GRANDAD GREW UP IN THE STREET NEXT TO THE GROUND, AND MY OTHER GRANDAD WAS A HUGE BLUES FAN—SO THERE WAS NO ESCAPE FOR ME!

IS IT TRUE THAT CHARLIE HAS THE SAME SURNAME AS A FAMOUS BIRMINGHAM CITY GOALKEEPER?

HERE I AM IN MY BLUES AWAY KIT. (NOTE THE CLASSIC POSE!)

YES, GIL MERRICK! HE PLAYED IN GOAL FOR BIRMINGHAM (1939-60) AND ENGLAND (1951-54). THEN HE BECAME THE BLUES' MANAGER AND LED THE TEAM TO WIN THE LEAGUE CUP!

DID YOU PLAY FOR A TEAM WHEN YOU WERE YOUNGER?

I PLAYED ONE SEASON FOR 'RAUNDS TIGERS'. THEN I FORMED A TEAM WITH MY MATES—A GROUP OF MISFITS LIKE NORTH STAR!

WHAT POSITION DID YOU PLAY?

I WAS QUITE A GOOD GOALIE, BUT AS WE GOT OLDER AND THE GOALS GOT BIGGER, I DIDN'T! EVERYONE SAID I WAS TOO SHORT TO GO IN GOAL, SO I MOVED TO RIGHT-BACK. OUTFIELD I WAS A BIT LIKE GERBIL: LOTS OF EFFORT, BUT NOT MUCH SKILL! (SORRY GERB!)

MORE

DID YOU ALWAYS WANT TO BE A WRITER?

NO, I WANTED TO BE A FOOTBALLER ... OR BATMAN!

WHEN DID YOU START WRITING?

I WANTED TO BE IN A BAND, SO THE FIRST THINGS I WROTE WERE SONGS. I'D COME HOME FROM SCHOOL AND DO GIGS FOR THE CAT!

WHAT WAS THE FIRST STORY YOU WROTE?

IT WAS A FOOTBALL STORY FOR A COMIC I DREW ABOUT A TEAM CALLED 'THE COMETS'. YOU CAN READ ONE OF MY EARLY COMET STORIES ON THE NEXT PAGE.

WHAT BOOKS DO YOU LIKE?

I READ LOTS OF DIFFERENT THINGS— CHILDREN'S BOOKS, TEEN AND YOUNG ADULT STORIES. I LIKE COMICS AND GRAPHIC NOVELS TOO.

WHAT ARE ALL THE PICTURES ON THE WALL ABOVE YOUR DESK? (SEE BACKGROUND IMAGE OF DAVE'S WORK ROOM.)

to tackle a moving train

THEY'RE A MIXTURE OF EARLY SKETCHES, DRAFT PAGES, REFERENCE PICTURES, AND INSPIRATION—LOTS OF BRYAN LEE O'MALLEY'S 'SCOTT PILGRIM' AND SATOSHI KITAMURA DRAWINGS. MY BIGGEST INSPIRATION THOUGH IS BILL WATTERSON WHO CREATED 'CALVIN AND HOBBES'. HIS CHARACTERS, STORIES, AND DRAWINGS ARE BRILLIANT. IF YOU'VE NEVER READ 'CALVIN AND HOBBES', FIND A COPY—NOW!

DAVE'S COMIC THIS WAY

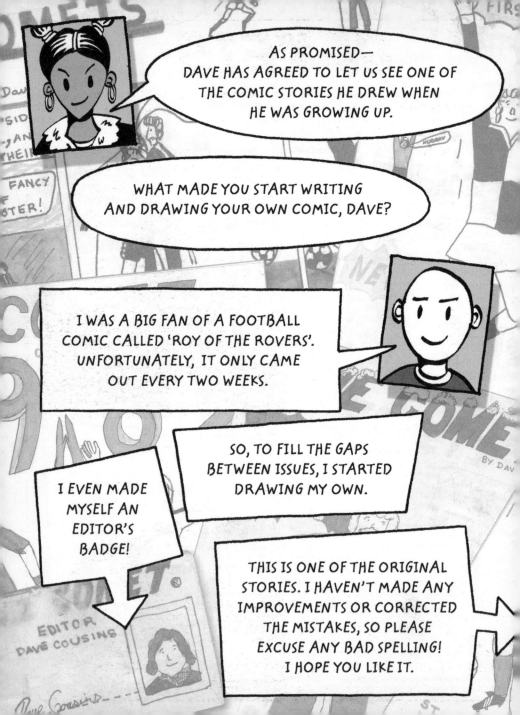

COMETS

WOODSIDE COMETS WERE A NEWLY FORMED YOUTH FOOTBALL TEAM. THEY WERE DESPERATELY TRYING TO GET INTO THE LOCAL LEAGUE. ANOTHER TEAM ALSO WANTED THE PLACE. TO DECIDE WHO WOULD PLAY IN THE LEAGUE A MATCH WAS ARRANGED BETWEEN WOODSIDE AND BARTON ROVERS. THE WINNERS WOULD GO INTO THE LEAGUE FOR THE FORTHCOMING SEASON.

IN THE DRESSING ROOM BEFORE THE MATCH....

AS THE TEAMS WALKED ONTO THE PITCH....

THE BARTON WINGER EVADED TWO TACKLES AND HEADED FOR COMETS GOAL.

BARTON KICKED OFF AND IMMEDIATELY THEY MADE THEIR POINT

MIKE STONE MADE A DESPERATE TACKLE

THE REFEREE WAS IN NO DOUBT...

PENALTY

OH, REF...

A BARTON STRIKER STEPPED FORWARD......

AND SHOT...

DAVE STOKES FLUNG HIMSELF ACROSS THE GOAL.....

AND PUSHED THE BALL ONTO THE POST. QUICKLY JON MITLER CLEARED THE LOOSE BALL.

A BARTON PLAYER COLLECTED THE LOOSE BALL AND....

1 - 2 -

BUT ONLY AS FAR AS BARTON'S No. 8, WHO BELTED THE BALL BACK IN, AGAIN DAVE GOT A HAND TO IT.

THE RAIN BEGAN TO FALL AS ANDY STEVENS PUT THE BALL ON THE CENTRE SPOT.

THIS WAS THE LAST ISSUE I DREW, SO I NEVER FOUND OUT HOW THE MATCH ENDED. MAYBE YOU COULD FINISH THE STORY, AND LET ME KNOW BY VISITING MY WEBSITE: WWW.DAVECOUSINS.NET.

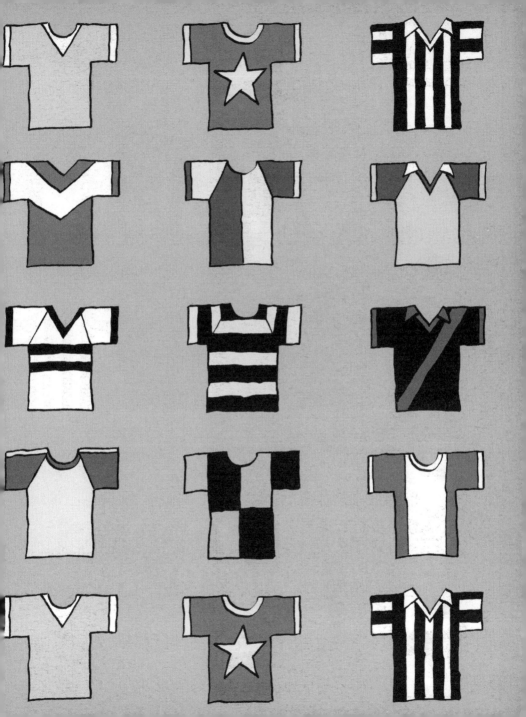